JODI:

The Secret of the Alaskan Gift

by
Virginia Work

MOODY PRESS
CHICAGO

© 1983 by
THE MOODY BIBLE INSTITUTE
OF CHICAGO

ISBN:0-8024-0274-7

1 2 3 4 5 6 7 Printing/LC/Year 88 87 86 85 84 83

Printed in the United States of America

Contents

The Words of My Mouth

Oh, the words of my mouth!
   The words of my mouth!
  Are they dirty or clean,
  Are they kind or mean?
Do they lift up to God,
    or drag down,
       down . . .

What kind of seeds have I sown?
   Strife, and slander,
     and impurity?
  Jealousy, pride,
     and sensuality?
Or have I sown gentleness,
    and joy from above?
Do my words bring peace,
    a gift of God's love?

Oh, the words of my mouth!
   the words of my mouth!
Set a watch on my lips, I pray, and
Help me to speak Thy words this day!

To my father and mother,
Vern and Gloria Stanton,
who have conquered the Alaskan wilderness
and have given me the inspiration for this book,
their encouragement, and their love

1

Mystery at the Airport

The giant silver bird hesitated on the runway, poised for flight. Puffy gray clouds were lifting after an early morning rain, leaving the grass glittering and the pavement black. Inside the big DC 737 there was a hush of expectation. Flight attendants, finished with their rounds of checking seat belts, scurried to their seats and clicked on their own belts.

Jodi Fischer, her red-brown hair curled softly around her pretty face and her sparkly blue eyes wide, sat clutching the armrests. MaryAnn Laine, her best friend, adjusted her seat belt nervously. Her large brown eyes were apprehensive, and she brushed her fingers through her short dark hair.

The plane began to move.

"Well, this is it!" Jodi said, leaning forward in her seat to watch the buildings zip past. "Alaska or bust!"

MaryAnn groaned softly. "Don't say that! What if it's bust?"

A tremendous thrust of power pressed Jodi back in her seat, and the roar of the jets filled her ears. The buildings were a blur now, and she felt the wheels thumping over the runway. Faster. *Faster*! She held her breath. And then—they were off! Beautiful, smooth, free flight! She let out her breath and smiled at MaryAnn.

"Man, this is neat!" she said.

MaryAnn shook her head. "I don't like take-off. Oh! Look down there!" Jodi leaned over to look out the small window. Below them spread out a maze of roads and miniature houses, schools, and swimming pools. Tiny cars, trucks, and buses swarmed on the streets like a nest of angry ants. The sun glinted on the silver wings of the jet as it banked in a wide turn.

"It's so neat your aunt and uncle invited us up to Alaska for two whole weeks!" Jodi said. "I wish it was for the whole summer! I've always wanted to go there! Just think, MaryAnn! The land of gold and mountains and maybe even boys!" She laughed. "Your uncle must be rich to pay our way!"

"Sh!" MaryAnn hissed as the lady in front of them glanced back and smiled. "Oh, Jodi! Can't you keep your voice down? You're going to embarrass me for sure!"

Jodi felt a flush spreading up from her neck. She looked down at her lap.

"Sorry, MaryAnn," she said in a low voice.

MaryAnn turned toward the window.

Jodi pulled a magazine from the pocket in front of her and swallowed. She knew those words were improper and spoken much too loudly. But why did MaryAnn always have to be right? She glanced over at MaryAnn's dark, shiny hair—cut in a new, short, blown-back style—and her slim, long-legged figure.

Jodi sighed. *It's just that I look so dumpy next to her,* she thought. *For once I'd like to have the money to dress like she does!*

She turned her thoughts to Alaska. The word sent shivers of excitement down her back. What was in store for her in that land of adventure? Was there another mystery around the corner?

The Please Fasten Your Seat Belt sign overhead flashed off with a *ding!* and people began unbuckling their seat belts and moving up and down the aisle. Jodi admired the pretty flight attendants' outfits as they served juice and coffee.

The man on Jodi's right reached for a magazine. He was small and dark-skinned with smooth, black hair slicked back from his forehead and a neat moustache. He wore a business suit and had a briefcase under the seat.

He glanced at her. "Bonjour, Mademoiselle."

"Hello!" Jodi replied with a smile. "Is this your first trip to Alaska? It's mine! My best friend's aunt and uncle invited us up for two weeks to visit. We're from British Columbia. My parents are missionaries to the Indian people. What do you do?"

He smiled vaguely. "You may say I am—how do you say—a businessman?" He spoke with a heavy accent.

"Oh, that's nice," Jodi replied. "What's your name?"

There was a slight hesitation. "Smith," he said. "Excuse me, please." With that, he stood and made his way down the aisle.

Jodi turned to MaryAnn. "Did you see that man?" she asked. "He's kind of funny."

"Did he use French?" MaryAnn replied, sipping her juice.

Jodi nodded. "Yeah. He must be from France, but he said his name was Smith. That isn't French, is it?"

MaryAnn grinned at her. "No, it isn't. Do you have a mystery already?"

Jodi rubbed her nose. "I don't know," she said slowly, The man returned to his seat, and she studied him carefully out of the corner of her eye. *If Smith isn't his real name, then it's a fake name,* she thought. *Why would he use a fake name?*

Just then a blonde flight attendant served them breakfast. Jodi bowed her head for a quick blessing and then began opening all the interesting little parcels on the tray. There were sausages, fluffy scrambled eggs, a bran muffin, a fruit cup, toast, orange juice, and a carton of milk. It was more than she could eat.

After breakfast, she and MaryAnn walked down the aisle to the tiny restroom, gazing out the windows at the snow-covered peaks on the right and the textured blue rug below them on the left.

"Hey, it's the ocean!" Jodi exclaimed. "Look at those islands, and that little fishing boat!"

Throughout the flight, Jodi kept watching for an opportunity to draw Mr. Smith into a conversation, but he sat with his head back and his eyes closed.

The Please Fasten Your Seat Belt sign dinged on, and the pilot announced they were on the final approach into the Anchorage International Airport. The plane dipped lower, and the flaps on the wings were lowered.

Jodi saw Cook Inlet below, dotted with fishing boats, and the skyline of Anchorage with its tall buildings. Dwarfing the city were jagged, snowy mountains. The jets were screaming in her ears now, and she gripped the armrests.

"We're landing in the water!" MaryAnn exclaimed, bracing herself, her brown eyes full of fear. "Oh! There's the runway!"

Jodi saw the pavement rushing up at them, and then felt a *thud* as the wheels touched. They were down!

Jodi let out her breath. "We made it, MaryAnn!" She glanced at her watch. "Twenty minutes early. Will your aunt and uncle be here to meet us?" She began gathering

10

up her purse and jacket.

MaryAnn nodded. "Oh, of course! I wonder how Stanley is. The last time I saw him, he was five and spoiled rotten!"

Jodi groaned. "That's all we need. A spoiled kid tagging along after us!"

MaryAnn laughed. "Well, that was eight years ago!"

Mr. Smith had straightened in his seat and was staring out the far window of the plane. He held his briefcase tightly in his hand. The moment the plane stopped, he was on his feet and down the aisle.

Jodi and MaryAnn stood and then pressed out into the aisle. Jodi strained to see where Mr. Smith had gone, but she lost him in the crowd.

Outside the plane the air was chilly. She slipped on her jacket and followed MaryAnn through a doorway and up the ramp into the airport.

"Are they here?" she asked MaryAnn. "Do you see them?"

MaryAnn peered through the crowd. "No, I don't. They must be here somewhere, though. Let's just keep looking."

Jodi hesitated in the wide hall, looking at each face that passed them. There were happy reunions and warm embraces all around, and she felt a little lonely and lost. Suddenly Mr. Smith walked by. She watched him intently.

He passed her without a glance, and she was about to point him out to MaryAnn when two men came up to him and began a conversation.

He shook his head as if he didn't understand. Then one grasped his arm and the other took his briefcase! He cried out and in one quick movement wrenched his arm free. Before the other two could stop him, he began run-

11

ning down the hall, weaving in and out among people. The other men gave chase.

"There they are!" MaryAnn cried out. "Hello, Uncle Howard and Aunt Phyllis!"

Jodi turned to see a woman approaching them. The man was slender with brown hair and eyes and wore glasses. The woman was rather heavyset, with stiffly styled blonde hair and a round face. The only resemblance she bore to MaryAnn's mother was her brown eyes.

"MaryAnn!" she cried, sweeping MaryAnn into her arms."You have grown so! And this is Jodi! It's so wonderful you girls could come!"

MaryAnn introduced Jodi.

Mr. Neilson smiled warmly and shook her hand. "I've heard a lot about you," he said, his eyes twinkling. "From all that MaryAnn has told us, I thought your name would be Nancy."

Jodi looked puzzled for a moment, and then she laughed.

"Oh, you mean Nancy Drew!" she exclaimed.

Mrs. Neilson sniffed. "I should hope not, Howard," she said. "We're going to have a nice, quiet visit. I can't wait to show you girls around Anchorage. You'll be surprised how much culture we have here! And real nice restaurants."

They began walking down the hall towards the baggage claim area, but Jodi paused beside a window, looking out over the parking lot. Something had caught her eye.

It was Mr. Smith, running from the building and hopping into a waiting taxi. The cab pulled away, and he was gone. *So Mr. Smith got away,* she thought, shaking her head. *I wonder what's going on.* Snapping out of her thoughts, she ran after the others.

Mr. Neilson was taking their suitcases off the revolving baggage receiver, and Mrs. Neilson was still talking.

"Stanley wanted to come, but he had a meeting to go to," she said. "He'll be home when we get there, probably back on that silly ham radio."

Jodi began listening. *Ham radio!* She grasped her suitcase and trailed along behind Mrs. Neilson and MaryAnn.

"Yes, he is such a bookworm too," Mrs. Neilson was saying. "I wish I could get him involved in some kind of sports. I did see—"

They were nearing the door that led outside, and Jodi suddenly saw the two men who had been chasing Mr. Smith. One was holding his briefcase. They were standing near the door, so she dropped to one knee to tighten her sandal strap.

"Well, that was rotten luck," one of the men said. He was balding and wore a suit.

The other man was large, had curly black hair, and wore jeans. He swore softly. "What's the boss going to say, Mac?" he asked. "That guy got away, and he knew where—"

"Shut up!" the older man snapped, looking straight at Jodi. "C'mon, let's get out of here!"

Jodi straightened, picked up her suitcase, and ran after Mr. and Mrs. Neilson. Mr. Neilson was hefting the suitcases into the trunk of their dark blue Cadillac, and Mrs. Neilson was chattering on about Stanley.

The constant flow of her words blended together until Jodi no longer heard them. She shivered with excitement as they drove out of the parking lot and down the streets of Anchorage. Why did those men want Mr. Smith? Who was "the boss"? What did Mr. Smith know that they didn't?

"My, you're the quiet one," Mr. Neilson said to her. She glanced at him.

MaryAnn laughed. "Jodi? Quiet? She's just up to something. Aren't you, Jodi? You've only been here for half an hour, and already you're digging up some mystery. Right?"

Jodi swallowed, feeling resentment at MaryAnn's words.

"I guess you're right," she replied. "But I'll probably never know what it's all about, so I might as well forget it." She gazed out the window. "Wow! Anchorage really is a big city!"

Mrs. Neilson nodded. "That's what I've been saying! We have everything here. After we take you home, and you freshen up some, we'll take you out to lunch at a nice restaurant. Is it too warm for you? We could have the air conditioner on."

Jodi shook her head. 'No, thanks! It was ninety when we left Seattle, and it's freezing here! Does it ever warm up?"

Mr. Neilson chuckled as he turned off the busy thoroughfare into a quiet residential area where the houses were far apart and luxurious.

"It gets up to eighty sometimes," he said. "But that feels hot to us." He made several more turns and then pulled into a long driveway and stopped in front of an attractive split level home. It sprawled elegantly on the natural curve of an immaculately kept lawn. To Jodi's surprise, there were bright splashes of color from the flower beds that adorned the smooth grass.

Inside, she caught her breath. The high ceilings with large cedar beams, the wide windows with their picture-framed views of Anchorage and the Inlet, the shag

14

carpets, and the modern kitchen all spoke of wealth and good taste.

"Would you like to see your room?" Mrs. Neilson asked. "This way." She entered a hall where there were steps going up and steps going down. "Stanley!" she called. "Come on down and greet our guests!"

A short, very slender boy about thirteen appeared at the top of the flight of stairs and leaped nimbly down them. He had brown hair like his father's and wore glasses. He had on a disheveled T-shirt and shorts, and his feet were bare.

"Here's MaryAnn, dear!" his mother said. "And this is her friend Jodi. Jodi, meet our son, Stanley."

Jodi nodded and smiled.

"Hi, Stanley," MaryAnn said. "Man, you've gotten taller!"

Stanley groaned. "How come all relatives have to say that! Hey, come on up to my room."

"That can wait," his mother replied, turning to go down the other flight of stairs. "The girls need to get settled, and then we're going out. Please put something more decent on, dear. You know I don't like that shirt!"

Jodi followed MaryAnn down the stairs and into the family room, where several couches flanked a large TV set. A pool table sat ready in another corner, and along one wall was a bar. There were sliding glass doors leading to a patio, and beyond that she saw the sparkling blue water in a swimming pool.

Their room was off the family room and was spacious with sliding glass doors leading onto the patio, a pink and lavender bathroom, twin beds, and a soft pink rug. Mr. Neilson carried in their luggage and left.

"I'll leave you to get settled," Mrs. Neilson said, fluttering around like a large, exotic butterfly. "If you need

15

anything, just ask. If it warms up this afternoon, you'll be able to go for a swim. Well, I'll see you later!"

Jodi took off her jacket and plopped down on the nearest bed.

"Whew!" she exclaimed. "What a house! And a swimming pool in Alaska! I can't believe it! But your aunt, MaryAnn! Does she ever stop talking? How does your uncle stand it?"

MaryAnn unzippered her suitcase and began hanging her clothes in the closet.

"You can have that bed," she said, ignoring Jodi's question. She opened a chest of drawers. "These are empty, so we can put our clothes in here. I'll take the top two, OK?"

Jodi shrugged. "OK. Did I hear your aunt saying something about a ham radio? I've been interested in them for a long time. Dad just got a CB for the van, and it's a lot of fun talking on it."

MaryAnn looked up from her unpacking. "Jodi, aren't you going to unpack and get changed? What time is it, anyway? I'm starved!"

Jodi glanced at her watch. "Just exactly noon," she said. "We lost two hours. It's only ten their time." She made a half-hearted attempt at unpacking.

MaryAnn began brushing her hair. "Do you think we'll meet any neat boys?" she asked, looking in the mirror.

Jodi frowned. "I don't need to worry. With you along, they'd never even see me." But she fished her brush out of her purse and brushed her fly-away curls. Then she turned to go.

"Let's go see Stanley's room," she said. "I'd like to see his ham."

MaryAnn knocked on Stanley's door a few minutes

16

later.

"Come in," Stanley called. Jodi stepped in behind MaryAnn and knew immediately that this was the room of a boy who got everything he wanted, and then some. It was very neat, and she gazed around at the models, the books on the shelves, the posters on the walls, and then at the big ham radio on a large desk. Behind it was a large map of the world with pins stuck in it.

"I got it for my birthday," Stanley said. "I had my license in two months, and that's a lot of work. You have to learn Morse code."

"Yeah, I know," Jodi said. "We have a CB in our van."

Stanley shrugged. "So do we—in Dad's truck. But ham is a different ball game! I can talk to people all over the world. Look. This is my log. These are the places I've contacted so far."

Jodi looked at his book and then leaned over and touched one of the dials on the radio.

"Hey! Don't touch that!" Stanley exclaimed sharply. "I had it set. Now I probably won't get that location again!" He sat down and turned the radio on, carefully moving the dial.

Jodi stepped back, a hot flush of embarrassment rising up her neck. *Spoiled brat is right!* she thought. Just then Mrs. Neilson called up the stairway for them to come.

Downstairs, Mr. Neilson handed MaryAnn a key. "This is for the front door," he said. "Whenever you leave, be sure to lock the door. There've been a lot of robberies around here recently."

MaryAnn nodded and put the key in her purse.

"We wouldn't need it to get in with, though," Jodi spoke up. "A guy back home showed me how to open locks with credit cards and pins!"

Stanley grunted behind her. "You better not let the

police know that. They'll be questioning you!"

"Whew!" Mrs. Neilson said as they went out to the car. "It's getting warm! Howard, please turn on the air conditioning. I just can't tolerate this heat!"

Jodi would have liked to leave her window open and let the warm breeze fan her cheeks and catch the smells of the city, but she rolled it up tight and shivered, wishing she had worn her jacket.

They drove down Northern Lights Boulevard and past the large bank where Mr. Neilson worked as vice-president. Then they turned off and headed away from the business district. Soon they were beside a small lake where Jodi could see dozens of small float planes tied up to docks. Several more were circling in the air, and others were out on the water.

"This is Hood Lake," Mr. Neilson said, slowing down and pulling into a small driveway. "Hundreds of float planes are here. There's a control tower, too, to direct air traffic." He stopped near a dock where a small blue and white plane bobbed in the water.

"Are you a pilot?" Jodi asked as they all got out and went to inspect the little plane.

Mr. Neilson nodded. "Almost everyone up here is. It's about the only way to get into a lot of the bush country. Mine is a Cessna one eighty-five. It holds three, plus the pilot."

"Yeah, and Dad is teaching me to fly," Stanley said. "I've flown it after we've taken off. I just haven't soloed."

"It's sure pretty," MaryAnn said, admiring the sleek little plane. "But I'm not so sure I'd want to fly in it."

Mr. Neilson smiled. "Oh, you'll like it. Some time this week I'll take you and Jodi up. How would that be?"

Jodi's blue eyes sparkled. "That sounds neat to me!"

Mrs. Neilson led the way back to the car, and they

drove through the city and then down near Cook Inlet where fishing boats were unloading their catches of salmon into long, rambling canneries.

"The silvers are running now," Stanley said. "Hey, Mom! Let's have the salmon Dad and I caught last week!"

His mother nodded. "Yes, dear." Then she continued talking. Mr. Neilson drove to a small but very attractive restaurant. Outside, there were smooth lawns with flowers and a pond with a footbridge over the water.

They were seated by a smiling hostess and given menus. After a little while, a young girl with straight black hair and dark slanted eyes came to their table and took a pen and pad from her apron pocket.

"Are you ready to order?" she asked without a smile.

Mr. Neilson glanced up. "Not quite."

Jodi watched as the young girl served another table. "Is she Chinese?" she asked.

Stanley snorted. "Chinese! She's Eskimo! You know, mushing dogsleds, and all the rest."

"Son," his father warned as the girl returned to their table. He looked at her. "Hello, Mikkel. I'd like you to meet some girls from Canada. This is my niece, MaryAnn, and her friend Jodi."

Still the girl did not smile, and Jodi saw that her dark eyes were red as if she had been crying recently.

Mr. Neilson glanced at MaryAnn. "Her father is a well-known artist. Isn't that right, Mikkel?"

Mikkel nodded. "I guess so, Mr. Neilson. Are you ready to order now?"

Jodi and MaryAnn followed Mrs. Neilson's lead and ordered tuna salad. Stanley ordered the French dip, and Mr. Neilson asked for the steak sandwich. The Eskimo girl took the order and hurried away.

"Something seems to be troubling her," Jodi commented. "I wonder what it is."

MaryAnn sighed elaborately, "Now don't go getting involved in everyone else's problems, Jodi!" she said. "We have lots of our own to handle!" Everyone laughed, but Jodi watched Mikkel, and once she was able to smile at her. Mikkel returned a faint smile and spoke to her.

That night, after a delicious dinner of stuffed salmon, fresh green salad, asparagus shoots with cheese sauce, and apple pie for dessert, Jodi crawled into bed, so tired she could hardly even mumble a good-night prayer. But her mind was busy with all that had happened that day. She saw all that she had said and done, and then she thought about the people she had met.

Would she ever find out about Mr. Smith? *Stanley.* Ugh! How could she stand two weeks of him? *Mikkel.* Something was troubling her! How could she help? She sighed and drifted off into an uneasy sleep.

2

A Scare in the Night

MaryAnn was calling her the next morning. Jodi stretched, got out of bed, and strolled over to the sliding glass doors to open the draperies. The early morning sun slanted across the lawn and touched the banks of flowers.

"Funny!" She yawned as MaryAnn put on the finishing touches of her make-up. "I never thought there would be flowers in Alaska!"

MaryAnn stood to go upstairs. "Well, this is the city. I don't imagine there are many out in the bush country."

Jodi got dressed, brushed her hair, and followed MaryAnn upstairs. Mr. Neilson had already left for work. Jodi sat down at the table and said a blessing silently while Mrs. Neilson served cantaloupe, fried eggs, bacon, and toast.

The phone rang, and Mrs. Nielson answered it. "Hello? Yes—yes, she is. Just a moment, please." She lowered the receiver and glanced at Jodi. "It's for you."

"Me?" Jodi exclaimed, glancing at MaryAnn with wide blue eyes. "Who would know me in Anchorage?" Rising, she took the receiver. "Hello?"

A woman's light, happy voice answered. "Hello, Jodi. This is Mrs. Holmes. I just got your mother's letter saying you were coming up here! Did you have a nice flight?"

Jodi smiled and relaxed, "Yeah. It was great. How did you know where I'd be staying?"

"Your mother wrote it in the letter," Mrs. Holmes explained. "When I got the letter this morning, I mentioned your coming to Mikkel, and she said she had met you last night in the restaurant."

"Mikkel?"

Mrs. Holmes chuckled. "The girl that waited on your table. She stays with us." Her voice sobered. "Jodi, I was wondering if you would do me a favor. Mikkel came to us recently because she's been having some problems. She really needs a friend her own age. She doesn't have any. And she said herself she would like to get to know you. I know you've just barely arrived, but I was wondering if you would mind if she came over for a visit this morning."

"Oh, sure!" Jodi exclaimed. "I kind of felt that something was wrong. Bring her on over!"

Mrs. Holmes hesitated. "Maybe I should talk to Mrs. Neilson to make sure it's all right with her."

"Sure! Here she is." Jodi handed the phone back to MaryAnn's aunt.

"Who was that?" MaryAnn asked as Jodi sat down beside her.

"Mrs. Holmes," Jodi replied. "We used to know them and work with them when they lived in British Columbia. They are missionaries to the Eskimo and Indian people here in Anchorage, and I think Mom said they run sort of a guest home. Anyway, Mikkel is staying with them, and she wants to come over and visit with us this morning. Isn't that neat?"

MaryAnn shrugged. "I guess so."

Mrs. Neilson replaced the receiver. "I'm going to have

22

to be gone this morning, girls," she said. "In fact, I have to run; I'm late already. Can you entertain Mikkel without me? I might not be back for lunch. There're cold cuts and rolls and whatever you can find in the refrigerator. Just put your dishes in the dishwasher." She hurried out of the kitchen.

"I just *knew* something was wrong when I saw her yesterday," Jodi said. She finished her juice and toast, as MaryAnn began clearing the table. "Mrs. Holmes says she's been having problems and she needs a friend."

MaryAnn glanced at her from the sink, frowning. "What kind of problems?"

"How should I know?" Jodi replied, bringing her dishes to the sink. "Why? What's the matter?"

MaryAnn shook her head. "This is supposed to be a holiday, Jodi," she exclaimed. "Why do we always have to borrow trouble and ruin everything? Can't we just enjoy and have a nice, peaceful time?" She sighed. "Oh, well, I guess it can't be helped with you along! Why don't you go straighten up our room while I finish here."

Jodi dashed from the room, angrier than she had been for a long time. Oh, the burning, scathing remarks she could hurl at MaryAnn! With strong, jerky movements she made her bed and hung her clothes. Then she took a deep breath and stood with her hands on her hips, anger still sparking from her blue eyes.

Who does she think she is! she thought. *The Queen of England? What a snob! Sometimes I just can't figure her out!*

She heard the doorbell ring and ran to answer it.

"Hi!" she exclaimed as she opened the door. An attractive, red-haired woman smiled back at her.

"Jodi! Hello!" she said, giving her a squeeze. "It's so good to see you! You've grown so much! You've met

23

Mikkel, I guess."

Jodi nodded and smiled at the short, dark-headed girl who stood behind Mrs. Holmes. "Hi, Mikkel," she said. "Come on in. Mrs. Neilson had to go out, but MaryAnn and I are here."

Mrs. Holmes stepped into the entryway and glanced around. "I can't stay, Jodi. My, what a lovely house!"

Just then MaryAnn came up behind Jodi. "This is MaryAnn, Mrs. Holmes. MaryAnn, meet Mrs. Holmes." They exchanged greetings, and then Mrs. Holmes turned to Mikkel.

"Just give me a call when you get ready to come home," she said with a smile. "Have a good time!" With a wave, she went back to her car and drove off.

Mikkel seemed nervous and tense as MaryAnn shut the front door.

"Would you like something to drink?" MaryAnn asked. Mikkel shook her head and dropped her eyes.

She's probably wishing she had never come, Jodi thought.

"Let's go down to the patio beside the pool," she suggested, leading the way through the kitchen and down the steps into the family room. "Isn't this a gorgeous house? And they have a swimming pool! You'll have to bring your swimming suit next time you come and go in with us."

"I don't know how to swim," Mikkel said in a low voice.

Jodi swallowed and opened the sliding glass doors, stepping out onto the patio. Mikkel and MaryAnn followed her and they all sat on the lawn chairs, watching the blue water twinkle in the morning sun.

Jodi chattered on and on about everything, and slowly Mikkel began opening up. When MaryAnn left to make some lemonade, Mikkel spoke of her past.

"We used to live in our little village," she said in a soft, musical voice that lifted the end of each sentence, making it sound like a question. "I really liked it there. But then my mother died, so we came to Anchorage so Daddy could find work."

Jodi nodded. "Mr. Neilson said he's a good artist. Do you paint, too?"

"A little," Mikkel replied, a tiny smile lifting the corners of her mouth. "I'd like to take an art course at the college here. That's what I'm trying to save money for." Her voice dropped even lower, and she almost whispered the rest. "I was, anyway. Until last night. Now I guess I'll never make it."

Jodi leaned forward and was about to ask Mikkel what had happened last night, when MaryAnn came back with the lemonade and some cookies on a tray, and the conversation shifted.

Finally Mikkel glanced at her watch. "I should be going," she said. "I promised Mrs. Holmes I'd do some ironing for her today."

"Did you want to use the phone?" MaryAnn asked, standing up.

Mikkel hesitated. "Well, I could walk. But—"

"I'll walk with you," Jodi put in, "I need the exercise."

Mikkel smiled at her appreciatively. "OK. It's not too far."

It felt good to be out and walking, but Mikkel seemed nervous and fearful. Several times she glanced over her shoulder, and after each time her steps quickened.

"Is there something wrong?" Jodi asked her after she had looked back for the third time.

Mikkel kept her eyes on the sidewalk. "No, not really. Well, there is something, but I can't tell you. Not here."

Jodi nodded and changed the subject.

They were practically running when they finally turned down the walk of a modern, two-story house.

Inside, Mrs. Holmes looked out of the kitchen as the girls came up a short flight of stairs.

"I could have come for you, Mikkel," she said, chuckling and sweeping her red hair back from her face. "Of course, the walk probably didn't hurt. I have to go shopping in a little while, and I can take you home, Jodi."

"I'll walk back, thanks," Jodi replied.

But Mrs. Holmes laughed and waved her hands, ducking back into the kitchen. "No problem. I'll let you know when I'm ready to go."

"Come on down to my room," Mikkel said, starting down a hallway.

Jodi followed her and stepped into a small, plain bedroom.

Mikkel shut the door firmly and then dropped her purse on the dresser.

In the very center of the dresser, leaning against the wall, Jodi saw an unframed painting. She stepped over to look at it up close. It was small, about the size of a piece of typing paper, but the picture caught her imagination. It was a swirling, howling snowstorm, so real she shivered without realizing it. In the center were two small Eskimo children, bundled up against the cold. The amazing thing was that they were not bent over, struggling against the wind to find shelter. They were rolling and laughing gleefully. In the middle of the storm, they were playing!

"This is really beautiful!" Jodi said sincerely. "Did your father paint it?"

Mikkel nodded. "He gave it to me the other day." She sat down on the bed and sighed. "I sure wish I knew where he went!"

Jodi turned to her. "Why? What happened?"

Sighing, Mikkel stood up and paced to the window. She glanced out and then yanked the curtains shut violently. For a moment she stood with her back to Jodi, her face in her hands and her shoulders shaking. Finally she straightened, fought down her sobs, and turned to Jodi.

"I'm sorry." she managed, reaching for a tissue. "It's just that everything is caving in on me, and I don't know what to do!"

Jodi perched on a chair. "Can—can you talk about it? Sometimes that helps a lot."

Mikkel nodded and plopped down on her bed. Still, it was a long time before she could tell her story. Finally it came, the words barely audible as her fingers twisted up little balls in the bedspread.

"When we came to Anchorage, Daddy got a job painting in a souvenir shop. It seemed like a good job at first, but his boss started demanding more and more of him. Like he was a machine that could mass produce paintings. You can't treat creativity like that. And he started drying up. Inside, I mean.

"Anyway, he left me just yesterday. I guess the pressure got to be too much. But I know he loves me, and he wouldn't just leave me without a good reason.

"And then last night I lost my job at the restaurant! So that leaves me with nothing. No family. No job. Nothing. I can't stay here forever, and I just don't know what to do!" She glanced up, and Jodi saw tears glistening in her eyes.

She opened her mouth to say something, but then she closed it. What in the world could she say?

"Well, God knows all about your problems, Mikkel,"

she said finally. "He will help you if you will turn to Him."

Mikkel shook her head. "I know. My daddy and I have been going to the Native Fellowship Church here in town. That's how I got to know the Holmeses. But, I don't know about it all. I guess I'm just not ready for that yet."

Jodi nodded. "Do you have any idea where your father could have gone?"

"No, he just left. He—this move to Anchorage wasn't so good for him. His big problem is drinking and gambling. And his friends, well, they were pretty rough. I think it has something to do with that." She looked at Jodi imploringly. "Will you not laugh if I tell you something else?"

Jodi shook her head. "Laugh! Why would I laugh?"

"Because it sounds so crazy!" Mikkel replied in a husky whisper. "Come here! Look!" She lifted a corner of the curtain, and Jodi peered out.

"Down there!" Mikkel whispered in her ear. "See that car? There're two men in it! They have been following me ever since Daddy left!"

Jodi stared out the window. Yes, she did see a car parked beside the curb not too far away. And, yes, it did have two men in it! Prickles of fear made goosebumps on her arms, and she let the curtain drop.

Mikkel paced back to the bed. "I just don't know what to do!"

"Well, I think I'd call the police!" Jodi exclaimed.

Mikkel whirled to face her. "No! I won't call the police! It's not that bad, Jodi. Really. I'll just have to wait and see what happens."

Jodi gazed at her, surprised. Why didn't she want to call the police? Was there something Mikkel hadn't told her? She frowned. "I think you should," she said slowly. "Or tell Mrs. Holmes at least."

Just then there was a knock on the door, and Mrs. Holmes looked in. "I'm ready to go, Jodi," she said. "Are you?"

Jodi nodded. "Sure."

"Could I come along, too?" Mikkel asked nervously. Jodi knew she didn't want to stay alone in the house while two strange men sat in a car outside.

"Of course," Mrs. Holmes answered and turned back down the hall.

Jodi stepped toward the door, but Mikkel stopped her. Picking up the painting from the dresser and thrusting it into Jodi's hands, she smiled faintly.

"Please, Jodi," she whispered. "I want you to have this."

"Oh, no! I couldn't take it!" Jodi exclaimed without thinking, pushing the painting back to the Eskimo girl. A hurt look came into Mikkel's eyes.

"Then—then you're not my friend," she said in a low voice.

Jodi grasped the painting and pulled it to her. "Oh, well, if that's—I mean, thanks, Mikkel. I really like it!"

Outside, they piled into Mrs. Holmes's red station wagon, and she backed out of the driveway. Mikkel turned her face away from the black car, but Jodi tried to see the men and the license plate. The men had their hats pulled low over their faces, though, and she missed seeing the numbers on the plates.

At the Neilsons' driveway, Jodi hopped out, thanking Mrs. Holmes for the ride and assuring her she could walk to the house. She turned and glanced down the street. Suddenly she froze, terror striking her heart! A black car had just driven by, very slowly, with two men in it! They had been looking at her!

She hugged tightly the painting Mikkel had given her. Then she saw the brake lights go on as the car slowed to a stop. Jodi began running. The house was a blur as she approached and pounded frantically on the door.

MaryAnn opened it. "Jodi! What in the world! You're as white as a sheet!"

Jodi pushed past her and slammed the door shut. Then she leaned against it and tried to catch her breath. "It—it was—that black—car again!" she gasped.

"*Car!*" MaryAnn replied sharply. "What are you talking about? There's hundreds of cars! Jodi, what's going on?"

Jodi sighed and led the way downstairs. She plopped down on her bed and sighed again.

"It's so crazy, MaryAnn. You're not going to believe it!" Then she told her friend all that she had seen at the airport, and about the men who had been following her and Mikkel.

MaryAnn listened, her brown eyes wide. "Leave it to you, Jodi!" she said, shaking her head. "I wonder what it means. Hey! Where did you get that painting? Let's see it!"

Jodi handed MaryAnn the painting and told her about Mikkel's problems. Then she set it carefully on top of the dresser.

That afternoon the temperature soared to eighty, so Jodi, MaryAnn, and Stanley went swimming. The twinkling blue water felt as good as it looked, and Jodi endured Stanley's teasing and bragging as much as she could. Finally she sprawled on one of the lounge chairs beside the pool, and MaryAnn flopped down beside her. Stanley sat with his feet dangling in the pool not too far away, occasionally sending a spray of water in their direction.

"Maybe if we ignore it, it will go away," Jodi said, turning away from him.

He sent another shower over her. "And maybe it won't," he said. "I don't know how you can stand all that religion stuff crammed down your throats. MaryAnn said your parents were missionaries! Ugh! Does your father wear a pith helmet and carry a big black Bible, Jodi?"

Jodi lifted up on her elbow. "Religion doesn't have anything to do with my relationship with Jesus," she said, her eyes spitting fire. "And I haven't ever had anything crammed down my throat!"

He laughed derisively. "Sunday school time, girls! That's just for babies! Intelligent people know there isn't a God! You've just been badly brainwashed!"

"You're not only a spoiled brat, you're a stupid one, too!" Jodi spat out.

Stanley leaped to his feet to dump some water on her, and she jumped up, tussling and fighting with him, finally pushing him over the edge into the pool.

Just then MaryAnn cried out. "Look!" she wailed, holding something up in her hand. "My watch! You clowns stepped on it! Look at it!"

Jodi stepped over to her, and Stanley pulled himself from the pool. Wiping her eyes, Jodi saw that the crystal had been smashed!

"Oh, MaryAnn!" she said. "I don't think I did it! I would have felt it under my bare feet!"

"I didn't do it, either," Stanley said, coming up behind her. "You shouldn't have left it on the patio, anyway!" He turned to Jodi. "And if you hadn't—"

"What good does it do to blame everyone else?" Jodi yelled. "One of us did it, and I'm willing to pay part of

31

the cost to get it fixed. I'm really sorry, MaryAnn."

MaryAnn shook her head, her brown eyes flashing. She gathered up her things and started for the door. "Just forget it." She stomped off into the bedroom.

Jodi picked up her towel, not daring to look at Stanley. Tears stung her eyes. It was childish to get into an argument with Stanley. But she had apologized, and what more could she do? Feeling guilty and miserable, she went to dress for dinner.

That night, Jodi sat stiffly at the dinner table, uncomfortable in a dress and hoping she wouldn't knock over her long-stemmed crystal glass. Mrs. Neilson talked on and on.

"Did you girls have a good day?" Mr. Neilson asked.

MaryAnn nodded, but she did not lift her eyes.

"MaryAnn's upset because she broke her watch," Stanley burst out.

MaryAnn looked up at him in surprise. "I—" She hesitated and then dropped her eyes once more.

"I don't think MaryAnn broke it," Jodi said slowly, toying with her food. "Stanley and I were goofing off, and it was stepped on. I said—"

"She shouldn't have left it on the ground!" Stanley interrupted, reaching for the butter. "It's not my fault!"

Mrs. Neilson patted MaryAnn's hand. "That's too bad, dear. We're not blaming anyone, Stanley. These things just happen. I'll take your watch down to the jeweler's tomorrow, MaryAnn. I have to go and pick up a clock I'm having repaired. It won't take long to fix, I'm sure."

Jodi cleared her throat. "I said I would help pay for it," she said. "Just let me—"

"Oh, my, no," Mrs. Neilson replied hastily. "I wouldn't hear of that, dear. Don't worry about it. It is just one of

32

those things."

After dinner, Stanley challenged Jodi to a game of pool in the family room.

"No, thanks," Jodi said. "I don't play very well."

Stanley laughed. "Chicken, huh! I'll go easy on you."

MaryAnn came up beside Jodi. "Thanks for offering to pay for my watch," she said. "I guess I was pretty mad."

"I don't blame you!" Jodi replied. She turned to Stanley. "Talk about chicken! Blaming MaryAnn for breaking her watch when you knew you had done it!"

"Aw, get off my back!" Stanley growled, smacking a ball into a pocket. "What a bunch of goody-goodies! You gotta look out for number one in this old world."

Jodi frowned. "It looks like you've been looked after too well!" she muttered.

"Oh, Jodi, just forget it," MaryAnn pleaded, turning on the television.

Jodi went to sit on the couch beside her, gritting her teeth and fuming inside.

That night, Jodi tossed and turned in her bed, unable to get to sleep. Her stomach felt like it was tied in knots, and her head throbbed. It wasn't just her problem with Stanley, although she felt guilty enough about that. Maybe it was the cold, formal feeling in this house. She rolled over again and thought of the men who had followed her and Mikkel. What did they want with her? Why were they following Mikkel?

She sighed and rolled over again. *Oh, well, maybe things will be better tomorrow,* she thought, drifting into a light sleep.

In her dream, MaryAnn was slowly opening a door and it was making a loud squeaking noise. Suddenly she was awake. She lay perfectly still, staring up in the darkness, and then she turned her head and looked toward the door. Convincing herself she had been dreaming, she rolled over and closed her eyes.

And then she heard it again. It was a noise—a squeaking, scraping noise somewhere nearby in the basement! She froze, her eyes staring wide. *What could it be?*

There it was again! Goosebumps covered her arms as she sat up. Should she wake everyone? What if it was something stupid, like boards contracting?

Her eyes had become accustomed to the darkness, so she stood and padded softly to the door of their room. Very slowly she opened it a crack and peeked out. All was still and empty.

Then she looked down the hall toward a door leading to another room. It slowly opened, and a dark shape appeared in the doorway!

3

Where Is the Painting?

Jodi screamed. She heard her voice echoing through the house. The door shut quickly and softly, and she crumpled against the doorsill and then to the floor. She heard MaryAnn's voice beside her and then steps pounding down the stairs.

"Jodi! What's the matter?" MaryAnn was saying in her ear. A light came on. "Oh, Uncle Howard. I'm glad you came down!"

"MaryAnn! Jodi! What is going on?" Mr. Neilson, wrapping a robe around his pajamas, came hurrying barefooted across the family room. "What was that noise?"

Jodi looked up. "Oh, Mr. Neilson!" she exclaimed, her blue eyes wide and her hair falling into her face. "I heard a noise and looked out the door, and I saw that door open and someone was coming out!" She pointed down the hall.

Mr. Neilson dashed to the door, flung it open, and turned on the light in the same motion. Mrs. Neilson thudded down the stairs, and behind her stumbled Stanley, pushing on his glasses.

"Howard!" Mrs. Neilson called. She had flung on her bright pink robe, and her hair was covered with a pink cap. "What is going on? Who was screaming?"

Jodi stood up. "I was," she said.

"That figures," Stanley snorted. "Only a dodo would—"

"Hush, son!" Mr. Neilson came back into the family room. "Someone broke in the workshop window! It's been jimmied open!" He glanced at his wife. "I'll call the police."

Mrs. Neilson gave a little shriek, and with her hand over her mouth she stumbled to the nearest couch and sank down on it.

MaryAnn rushed to wet a washcloth in the bathroom, and Stanley and Jodi stepped into the workshop to look at the window.

"Don't touch anything!" Jodi cautioned as he stepped closer to the window.

He turned to her angrily. "I know that! Why didn't you try to catch him? All you could do was stand there and scream! Girls!"

Jodi turned on her heel and went back to the family room. MaryAnn had laid the wet cloth on Mrs. Neilson's forehead.

"I'm all right now." she said, removing the washcloth and sitting up. "What a shock! To think—someone broke into our house, and Jodi stopped him! It's a good thing you're a light sleeper, Jodi! No telling what that man would have done!"

"So Jodi's the big hero now." Stanley sneered. "Maybe she's in with the crooks. Nothing like this happened before she came!"

Jodi frowned and clenched her teeth, feeling a hot rush of anger rising up her neck and onto her face. Hateful words swirled through her mind. But just then Mr. Neilson returned. "They'll be here in a few minutes," he said, pacing nervously. "Did you get a look at that man, Jodi?"

Jodi shook her head. "No, I didn't. I just saw the door opening and then a dark shape coming out. Was anything stolen?"

Mr. Neilson went into the workshop and came out a few minutes later.

"No, it doesn't look like it," he said. "He must have been after something more valuable."

"Howard!" Mrs. Neilson exclaimed. "I never dreamed this house would be so easy to break into! You must see about a good alarm system! I won't rest until one is installed!"

MaryAnn smiled. "As long as Jodi's here, we don't need an alarm," she said.

Jodi grinned sheepishly.

The doorbell rang, and Mr. Neilson brought two policemen down the stairs. They examined the window and questioned Jodi and Mr. Neilson. Then they left, saying they would call if they found out anything.

Everyone went back to bed, but it was a long time before Jodi got to sleep.

MaryAnn was shaking her the next morning, but she rolled over and groaned.

"Come on, sleepyhead!" MaryAnn called. "Breakfast is on, and Uncle Howard says he's going to take us up in his plane today!"

Jodi sat up. "Really? Oh, that's great!" She glanced at the calendar on the wall. *Wednesday! Twelve more days in Alaska!* She leaped out of bed and headed for the bathroom.

"I just hope Stanley stays home!" she called to MaryAnn. "I don't think I can stand much more of him!"

"Well, if you'd just learn to keep your mouth shut!" MaryAnn called in to her. "I'm going up to help. Hurry!"

It was a cloudless, sunny day. The sky was a deep, turquoise blue, and the mountains were stark and rugged against it. Jodi took a deep breath of the clear air as she stepped from the car at Hood Lake. Her heart was singing. Mr. Neilson was taking them flying, and Stanley wasn't coming!

Mr. Neilson wore hip boots and a billed cap. He whistled as he checked the little blue and white Cessna inside and out, filled it with gas, and pumped out the floats.

"Do they leak much?" Jodi asked, holding onto one of the struts as she watched him.

He smiled up at her. "No, not much. Just enough to make me pump them out once in a while. Now, who would like to sit up front?"

Jodi looked at MaryAnn, and MaryAnn laughed as Mr. Neilson climbed into the plane.

"Go ahead," she said, giving Jodi a gentle push.

Jodi smiled. "Thanks, MaryAnn. I'll let you next time." She let MaryAnn get into the backseat, and then she stepped up on the float.

"Just untie us from the dock," Mr. Neilson said. "Then give the dock a push while you stand on the float. That's right. Here you go." He gave her his hand, and she climbed into the plane and shut the door.

"It seems so *small*!" MaryAnn commented from the back. "I don't know about this!"

Jodi fastened her seat belt. "I know!" she said, smiling. "I know I'm going to love it!"

The motor sputtered to life, and the propeller whirled in front. Mr. Neilson worked some levers and turned the plane around. Jodi looked at all the dials and instruments. He requested permission for takeoff from the control tower, permission was granted, and the motor roared in their ears. They skimmed over the water, and Jodi held her breath without realizing it.

Mr. Neilson pulled back on the controls, the plane swooped up, and they were off! Jodi laughed at MaryAnn's pained expression and pointed to the city of Anchorage spread out below them.

Leaving the city and turning southeast, they flew over the jagged Chugach Mountains that formed the backdrop for Anchorage, and below them was a streak of silver water and a blacktopped highway.

"This is the Turnagain Arm of the Cook Inlet," Mr. Neilson explained over the noise of the motor. "Down this way is Kenai and Seward, where they do a lot of fishing. We won't go that far. I just wanted to show you a glacier."

"It's beautiful!" Jodi yelled back.

He nodded, smiling. "Just wait."

The mountains towered up on both sides now, and they flew down the valley. After a while, she noticed that the snow on the mountains looked different—it was tinted blue.

"Glacier ice!" Mr. Neilson called out, pointing to the huge masses of ice clinging to the sides of the mountains.

The valley widened, and at the far end Jodi could see an enormous field of snow, miles and miles of sparkling whiteness blanketing the mountain passes. At the foot of the snowfield was a small turquoise lake with dozens of icebergs floating in it.

"Portage Glacier!" boomed Mr. Neilson. "At one time it filled this whole valley!" He glanced back at MaryAnn.

Jodi nodded, unable for once to speak. The absolute grandeur and beauty of it all took her breath away. It seemed she could reach out and touch those rugged peaks, garnished with their globs of blue glaciers, and the green of the foliage below them. She took in the beauty of the lake with its Popsicle-blue icebergs, and the immensity and wrinkled whiteness of the glacier itself with its deep blue crevasses.

Tears sprang to her eyes, and in that moment she lost her heart to Alaska.

Mr. Neilson banked the plane and turned from the glacier.

"Where are we going now?" MaryAnn asked, leaning forward.

"Thought I'd take you over the Matanuska Valley, and we might see Mount McKinley from there," he replied.

"Oh, I hope we can see it!" Jodi exclaimed, her eyes sparkling. "Just think, the highest peak in North America!"

"I've heard a lot about the Matanuska Valley, too," MaryAnn said. "That's where they grow those *big* cabbages!" She spread her arms wide, and Jodi laughed with her.

They followed a strip of brown, roily water that spread out over a wide river bed. The mountains were farther away now, and the wide valley below was dotted with farms.

"That's the Matanuska River," Mr. Neilson commented. "It comes from a glacier, too. It's full of silt."

"How many glaciers are there in this country?" MaryAnn wanted to know.

He chuckled. "Plenty."

They turned east of the valley, and the land below them looked like a green rug that was dotted with hundreds of small lakes and striped with rivers. A busy little town made an oasis in the green foliage, and then they followed another wide, brown river.

"That's the Susitna River," Mr. Neilson told them. "Now, look up that way. I think the clouds are clearing. You should be able to see Mount McKinley."

Jodi stared ahead to the north. On the horizon, far away, she could see snow-covered peaks. The clouds drifted away, and then she could see one huge mountain, towering into the sky and dwarfing everything around it.

"There it is!" she exclaimed. "Mount McKinley! Isn't it big!"

"Wow!" MaryAnn exclaimed. "It looks like a monstrous ice cream cone! What are those mountains beside it, Uncle Howard?"

"That's the Alaska Range," Mr. Neilson said. "How do you like Alaska now?"

"I love it!" Jodi said, grinning. "I wish I could get on the ground and see what it's really like!"

Mr. Neilson studied the ground below for a few minutes.

"Well, I'm ready for a cup of coffee, and I know some real nice people who live on a lake up here. See that one with all the islands? It's called Lucy Lake. Shall we land?"

"Sure!" both girls called out together.

Mr. Neilson circled the lake, and they could see several cabins built along the shore. The main highway to Fairbanks ran along one side of the lake. The turn completed, Mr. Neilson brought the plane down for a smooth landing on the far side. They taxied up to a dock where several boats were tied.

A tall boy about seventeen stood on the dock.

"This looks interesting," MaryAnn commented. Mr. Neilson smiled. Jodi studied the boy as they came up.

He was good looking. The wind from the props blew his golden brown hair. He was smiling, and then when

41

the plane approached, he grabbed the wing tip and guided the plane to the dock and tied it up.

"Hello, there!" Mr. Neilson called as Jodi opened the door.

The boy looked up, and she found herself looking into laughing, hazel eyes.

"Hi," she said, grasping the struts and pulling herself out. "I'm Jodi."

He smiled and said hello.

Mr. Neilson scrambled out feet first, and then Mary-Ann slowly climbed out.

"Girls, this is Jay Evans," Mr. Neilson said, readjusting his cap. "Jay, this is my niece, MaryAnn Laine, and her friend Jodi Fischer from British Columbia."

He grinned at them, and Jodi admired his dark tan and broad shoulders. Just then a tall, graying man came out on the dock. He shook hands with Mr. Neilson and was introduced to Jodi and MaryAnn as Mr. Evans. He had sharp brown eyes, a prominent nose, and a big smile.

"Come on up to the cabin," he said. "I think we can rustle up a cup of coffee." They followed him up the hill, and Jodi heard Jay asking MaryAnn a question. She glanced back and saw MaryAnn blushing and running her fingertips through her dark hair.

Mr. Neilson held the door for Jodi. "He built this cabin himself," he said.

Jodi gazed at the softly glowing logs tightly wedged together and nodded. "It's a beautiful cabin," she said.

Mr. Evans smiled. "Thank you. This is my wife. Dear, this is Mr. Neilson's niece, MaryAnn, and her friend Jodi from British Columbia."

Mrs. Evans was grandmotherly with soft, white hair and bright blue eyes. She hugged both girls, and Jodi liked her at once.

They were ushered into the living room. Along one wall was a couch made from birch logs, and next to that, on the wall, was a citizen's band radio. Jodi could hear the low chatter of talk coming from it. She sat on a low stool near the window and then saw Jay and MaryAnn going back down the trail to the lake!

She was about to follow them when Mr. Neilson asked a question that stopped her. Slowly she sank back down on the stool.

"What about all the robberies on the lakes out this way?" Mr. Neilson had asked.

Mr. Evans shifted in his chair. "I don't like it, that's for sure. It used to be that you could trust everybody, and you could leave your cabin open for the next guy to use. He would leave it replenished with wood and food if he could." He paused. "But those days are gone, I'm afraid."

"What robberies?" Jodi couldn't resist asking.

Mr. Evans turned to her. "There have been a lot of break-ins on the lakes recently," he told her. "Especially where people build weekend cabins. The thieves will fly in, see if anyone is around, and steal whatever they can get in their planes. Then they're gone. It's hard to catch them."

"Has there been any trouble here?" Mr. Neilson asked.

"Not yet," Mr. Evans replied, shaking his head. "I've seen a strange red plane several times, but it takes off before I can get close to it."

Mr. Neilson paced to the window. "Too bad they can't be caught," he said. "But I suppose by the time you call the police, they're gone."

They spoke a little more about the strange plane and then began talking about flying. Jodi wandered out to the kitchen. On the wall she saw a Bible verse and on the end of the counter was a Bible.

Mrs. Evans smiled at her as she kneaded bread dough. "How long are you staying in Alaska?" she asked as Jodi sat down at the table.

"Just two weeks," Jodi said. "I wish I could stay longer. This is beautiful country. Are—are you a Christian?"

Mrs. Evans beamed. "Why, yes! You are, too, aren't you?"

Jodi nodded. "My folks are missionaries to the Indian people. Of course, that doesn't make me a Christian, but—"

"But it's a wonderful thing to be raised in a Christian home, Jodi," Mrs. Evans finished for her. "Does Mary-Ann know the Lord?"

Jodi nodded. "Yes, but I don't think her aunt and uncle do. They're nice, but it's so different in their home." She paused. "I guess I'm getting homesick already."

"Why don't you come out and stay with us for a while?" Mrs. Evans paused in her kneading to look at Jodi with bright eyes.

"Oh, that would be neat!" Jodi exclaimed.

Just then Mr. Neilson came into the kitchen. "I think we should be heading for home. Thank you for the coffee, Mrs. Evans. I can't ever resist stopping at Lucy Lake!"

Mrs. Evans laughed and brushed off her floury hands. "Well, you know you're always welcome. We were thinking it might be nice if the girls could come out and stay a couple of days with us. That is, if you could spare them."

Mr. Neilson nodded. "It sounds OK to me," he said. "We'll see what MaryAnn says."

Jodi followed the others down to the dock, frowning. *What are Jay and MaryAnn doing? Why couldn't they have asked me to go along?*

MaryAnn scrambled out of the large motor boat where she and Jay had been sitting and said that she certainly *would* like to visit at the Evanses'! Jay's eyes lit up happily, and he smiled at her.

A little later, Jodi leaned back in her seat as the small plane lifted off the water. They circled over the Evanses' cabin and waved from the windows. Three small figures on the dock waved back. Then they headed for Anchorage.

But somehow, the joy Jodi had felt that morning was gone, and her heart was cold. Even small-plane flying over Alaska did not thrill her now. She watched the countryside unfold below like a 3-D movie, and occasionally she glanced at MaryAnn in the front seat. *Neat, beautiful, slim MaryAnn!* she thought bitterly. *What chance do I stand beside her?*

They arrived in Anchorage, and Mr. Neilson requested permission to land on the lake. Permission was granted, and they dropped down to the water. It was a smooth landing, and soon they were tying up at the dock. MaryAnn, her brown eyes shining, was chattering excitedly about how much she liked flying and how nice the Evanses were.

Jodi turned away and watched another plane take off and two land. The last one to land taxied up to a dock nearby, and Mr. Neilson waved to the pilot. Tall and dark, he came over to them with a big smile.

"Jodi, MaryAnn, this is Mr. Burke," Mr. Neilson said. "He owns two gift shops downtown. Mr. Burke, this is my niece and her friend visiting from Canada."

Mr. Burke seemed to size them up in one flash of his

sharp blue eyes. They were flinty hard, and for a second Jodi shivered. But then his words and laugh made her relax.

"Hello, girls," he said, raising his eyebrows. "How do you rate, Neilson? Finding two pretty girls! Have you been up sight-seeing? How do you like Alaska?"

"It's great!" Jodi grinned. "I'd like to stay up here forever!"

Mr. Burke laughed heartily. "Well, listen," he drawled, digging in his shirt pocket. "You girls go on over to the Gold Nugget Gift Shop and get something on the house." He signed his signature on two of his calling cards and wrote five dollars on the back of each. Then he handed the cards to Jodi and MaryAnn.

"Thanks!" Jodi said. "I've already got a painting by an Eskimo man that is really nice. Maybe you know Mikkel and her father. She—"

"Mikkel Pokiak?" Mr. Burke asked sharply.

Mr. Neilson nodded. "I introduced her to them the other day."

"I understand her father ran away," Mr. Burke went on. "He used to work for me. I'd sure like to get him back. The customers are asking for his paintings. Did Mikkel tell you where he might have gone?"

Jodi shook her head. "No, she said she wasn't even going to look for him. Maybe he went back to their village."

Mr. Burke rubbed his chin. "Could be. Well, I have to be going. If you find anything out about him, let me know."

"Sure," Jodi said. They told Mr. Burke good-by and got into the Cadillac. Her talk with him had raised all the old questions. *How can I help Mikkel? Why did her father run away? Who was following her, and why?*

She was suddenly jolted out of her thoughts when the car swerved violently, and she caught a glimpse of an old rattle-trap pickup whizzing by, scarcely missing them.

Mr. Neilson slowed to a stop and shook his head. "That was close!" he said, wiping his forehead. "I wish I'd gotten his license number!"

"I got a look at him," MaryAnn commented. "He had dark hair and a moustache." She glanced at Jodi. "In fact, he almost looked like your friend on the plane."

Jodi sat up, instantly alert. "You mean Mr. Smith? But what would he be doing around here?"

They arrived home and Jodi went to her room, still thinking hard. She tossed her things on her bed and glanced at the dresser.

"Hey!" she said suddenly. "*My painting! It's gone!*"

4

A Fishy Ordeal

"What are you yelling about now?" MaryAnn asked, coming into the room.

"My painting!" Jodi exclaimed, leaping over to the dresser. "The one Mikkel gave me! It's gone!" She began searching the floor and dresser.

"Are you sure you left it here, Jodi?" she asked. "You didn't put it in your suitcase?"

Jodi shook her head. "No, you saw it yourself, and I haven't touched it since."

Together they searched the room, opening the dresser drawers and even moving it away from the wall. Jodi opened her suitcase to satisfy MaryAnn. But the painting was gone.

"Come on, Jodi," MaryAnn said, "let's go ask Aunt Phyllis. Maybe she was cleaning in here or something and moved it."

Jodi followed her up the stairs and into the kitchen. Mrs. Neilson was talking on the telephone, but then she hung up.

"Hello, girls," she said. "How did you like flying?"

Jodi tried to smile. "Oh, it was neat. Did you—"

"Aunt Phyllis," MaryAnn interrupted. "Jodi was given a painting, the one of the Eskimo children playing in the snow, and she put it in our room on the dresser. Just now, when we went in the room, we noticed it wasn't there, and we've looked everywhere and can't find it. I was wondering if you had seen it."

Mrs. Neilson frowned. "No, I haven't, MaryAnn. Surely it's in your room somewhere." She led the way down the stairs, and once more they searched the room.

Finally she straightened up from looking under the bed and patted her hair.

"Whew! It isn't under there!" She stood and went to the door. "Stanley! Stanley! Come on downstairs for a moment!"

A few minutes later, Stanley appeared, looking upset at being interrupted in what he had been doing.

"What do you want?" He frowned.

Mrs. Neilson told him about the missing painting and asked if he had seen it or knew what had happened to it. But he shook his head.

"No, I haven't seen the crummy thing. Did you call me for that?" He shot a glance at Jodi. "Can't she keep track of her things?"

"Now, Stanley." Mrs. Neilson scolded mildly. "Did you go out this morning, dear? Or did anyone come in?"

Again the brown-haired boy shook his head. He pushed his glasses up on his nose and turned to the door.

"The only one who was here was Mrs. Toye. I don't know who would want a picture of a snowstorm anyway!" He left the room.

Mrs. Neilson sighed and led the way back to the kitchen.

"I'll call Mrs. Toye," she said, dialing a number, "but I'm sure she wouldn't take anything. She's been our housekeeper for years, and I know—oh, hello, Mrs. Toye." She told the cleaning lady about the painting and asked if anyone had come to the door, or if she had seen anyone around.

"A man?" her voice squeaked, and she sat down on a stool. "Outside? Oh. Yes, I see. What did he look like, Mrs. Toye? Yes, yes. OK. Thank you." She hung up and turned to Jodi and MaryAnn with a puzzled expression on her face.

"She saw the painting in your room," she said nervously. "But no one came to the door. Just as she was leaving, however, she saw a man coming down the driveway. She saw him going to the side of the house and assumed he was the meter reader."

"What did he look like, Mrs. Neilson?" Jodi asked breathlessly, leaning forward, her blue eyes like saucers.

"Dark. That's what she noticed—dark. And he had a moustache."

Jodi looked at MaryAnn and shivers went down her spine.

"It must have been—" She gulped. "Mr. Smith! He must have stolen my painting! But why?"

"And how did he get it?" MaryAnn put in.

"That's a good question!" Mrs. Neilson commented, reaching for the phone. "I'm calling Howard. Surely Stanley would have heard someone breaking in! Oh, my head!" She sank down on the stool, and Jodi and MaryAnn went back to the family room.

"This is what I would call a real mystery now, MaryAnn!" Jodi exclaimed, sinking down on the brown couch. "Mr. Smith must have gotten that painting somehow! But how? Do you think Stanley would have heard him with those head phones on?"

Suddenly she sat up. "Hey! I just thought of something! We never showed that painting to Stanley, and yet he knew what it was! He must have had something to do with it!"

MaryAnn sighed and picked up a magazine. "Oh, Jodi. Maybe he came in our room and saw it!"

Jodi shook her head. "But why would he go in our room?"

Stanley popped around the corner and leaped down the steps into the family room. He frowned at Jodi.

"So I'm suspect number one, huh? Wouldn't you like to read my mind right now!"

"No, I wouldn't!" she replied flatly, turning away.

He flashed her an angry look.

"Come on, Jodi," MaryAnn said, starting for the door. "Let's go for a swim before dinner."

Jodi followed her to the door of their bedroom, frowning at Stanley.

"You'll never find out from me!" Stanley mocked her and hit a ball into the pocket of the pool table.

Jodi swung around and slammed the door.

The water was cool and refreshing in the swimming pool, and soon she climbed out and sprawled on a lounge. But a cloud covered the sun, and suddenly she was cold. Back in the bedroom, she put on a warm sweater and jeans, and then sat on her bed, blowing her hair dry and puzzling about the mystery.

That Stanley! she thought, coming back again and again to the missing painting. *Why does he have to be so rotten?* She sighed. *Oh, Lord, help me to be kind to that kid!*

Jodi paced around the room restlessly and thought about Mikkel. Maybe she had heard from her father! She certainly should tell her about the stolen painting. She strapped on her sandals and went upstairs.

"MaryAnn?" she called, glancing into the kitchen. MaryAnn sat at the kitchen table writing on post cards. No one else was around. "I'm going over to visit Mikkel.

Be right back."

MaryAnn lifted her eyebrows. "Do you know the way? You'd better not be late for dinner. Aunt Phyllis insists that everyone is here on time!"

"I'm just going for a short walk, MaryAnn," Jodi replied, her voice rising. "I'll be back." She ducked out the door and strode down the drive.

As she approached the Holmeses' house, she began looking fearfully at the cars parked along the sidewalk. Would that black car still be here? Was Mikkel still being followed? But there were no black cars. A strange blue Volkswagen bug was in the driveway, and the Holmeses' red station wagon was gone. She pushed the doorbell in relief.

Mikkel answered. "Oh, Jodi!" She smiled. "It's you. Come on in. No one is here but me. Did you want to see Mrs. Holmes?"

"No, I wanted to talk to you," Jodi told her, stepping inside as Mikkel leaned over and tied on a shoe.

"Are you going somewhere?"

Mikkel flashed her a smile, and Jodi was surprised at how friendly and lighthearted she seemed. She spoke in her musical, lilting voice.

"I just got a call from a friend of my father's," she said. "He works on one of the fishing boats, and he lets me drive his car when he's out. He says there's an opening at a cannery. Come along, OK? I could show you the canneries and fishing boats. It's really neat, OK?" She finished tying her shoes and straightened up.

Jodi hesitated. "It won't take long, will it? I have to be back by five-thirty. That's when the Neilsons have dinner."

"Come on," Mikkel said as she locked the front door. They went to the Volkswagen and got in.

"Have you seen that black car around?" Jodi asked as they drove down the street.

Mikkel shook her head. "No, I haven't. It left the day you were here and hasn't been back. I'm glad!"

After they had driven for a short time, Jodi noticed that after every turn, Mikkel glanced in her rearview mirror. Finally she shook her head.

"I think we're being followed," she said softly. They stopped at a red light, and Jodi looked back at a small foreign car. She caught a glimpse of a dark-haired man behind the wheel.

"That's Mr. Smith!" she exclaimed. "He almost crashed into us today! He was on the plane when we came! I think—"

"He doesn't know Anchorage like I do, then," Mikkel said and swung the car sharply around a corner. "I think I can lose him."

She turned again and, stepping on the gas, ducked down another alley, zipped through a shopping center parking lot, out into another street, and quicker than Jodi could think she pulled into a service station and then screeched through an open garage door.

Mikkel jumped out and pulled down the door. Jodi, her blue eyes wide with fright and her fingers stiff from gripping the armrest, watched her as a man approached her angrily.

"What are you doing?" he asked. "Someone could have been killed! What do you want, anyway?"

Mikkel glanced around, bewildered, and shrugged. "Wrong garage! Sorry!" The man opened the garage doors, shaking his head, and with a wave she backed the car out.

Jodi let go of the armrest. "Wow! Did—did you lose that Mr. Smith?"

Mikkel checked the rearview mirror and chuckled. "I think so. Let's go on down to the docks."

A salty sea spray and the cries of gulls wheeling above the long, low canneries greeted Jodi when they stepped out of the car a little later. Mikkel led the way past several buildings and stepped through the open doorway into a cannery. Jodi followed her.

She was in a small room where several men sat around a table, drinking coffee and talking. A tall, slim man with long dark hair caught up in a pigtail on his neck nodded to them.

"Come with me," he said shortly. He led them through another door into the cannery itself. Jodi followed behind Mikkel.

"This is where the fish is packed," Mikkel said, motioning toward rows of women who stood in front of large pans of salmon steaks and with deft movements were stuffing them into small cans. They walked past noisy machinery where the salmon was sealed into the cans and pressure cooked. Men were packing the cans into boxes at the rear of the cannery, and the boxes were stacked up, ready for shipping.

They stepped out the back door onto wooden planking and saw the boats with their tall masts, their fishing nets drawn up in spools, and their yawning holds where the salmon was held.

The man with the pigtail led them down the wooden planking toward a small boat tied to the dock. He stepped over the side of the boat. Jodi glanced at her watch. *Five-ten!*

"Mikkel!" she exclaimed. "I have to get back right away!"

"This won't take long, Jodi," Mikkel said over her shoulder as she clambered onto the boat and hurried after the man. "Come on!"

Jodi hesitated and then took a step towards the boat, but she tripped on a rope lying on the dock. Catching the side of the boat, she stepped over the side and glanced around. *Mikkel was gone!*

"Wait up!" she called, heading for the small cabin at the far end of the boat. But then suddenly she was grabbed from behind! Dirty hands that smelled of tobacco and fish covered her mouth and strong arms circled her like a vise.

She struggled, but the man lifted her off her feet and she was falling. She tried to scream and flailed out with her arms to catch herself. And then she landed. But instead of hard wood, she was on something wet and slimy. A door overhead banged shut.

"Ugh! Fish!" In rising panic, she tried to stand up and reach the door above her head, but there was no way she could get to her feet in the pile of fish.

Finally, after rolling around and getting wet and tired out, she lay still and caught her breath. Oh, the smell! She almost gagged.

"Oh, Lord!" she gasped. "I guess I know how Jonah felt!" She paused and wiped the slime from her face. "Dear God, please help me out of this mess!"

She reached out in the darkness and felt something solid. It was the side of the boat, and there were pieces of wood nailed to it. Slowly she grasped the wood and pulled herself up. Then with one free hand, she banged on the side of the boat and yelled until she thought her lungs would burst.

Suddenly there was a noise, and a man's face was framed in the hole above her.

"Is someone down here?" he called.

"Help me!" Jodi croaked, reaching up her hand.

"Someone pushed me in here!"

"Just a minute," the man said and disappeared. The minutes ticked off slowly, and Jodi wondered if he had forgotten about her. Then he was back, lowering a rope into the hold. She grasped it, and the man pulled her out.

She rolled onto the deck. "Oh, that was awful!" she moaned, sitting up. "Thank you so much!"

He reached down and helped her stand.

She looked at him in the soft twilight of the setting sun and gasped. *It was Mr. Burke!*

5

At Lucy Lake

"Mr.—Mr. Burke!" Jodi stuttered. "What are you doing here?"

He laughed. "I see it's Mr. Neilson's little friend! I might ask the same question. I was on my way to my boat." He gestured down the planking. "I do a little fishing on the side. So you were getting acquainted with Alaska's richest resource!" He laughed again, but she didn't think it was funny.

"It's the smelliest, too," she said, running her fingers through her damp hair. "Who would push me in there? I think we should call the police! And where did Mikkel go? I came down here with her."

He helped her over the side of the boat and stood near her, holding her arm. His sharp, blue eyes flashed up and down the dock for a second as if he were looking for someone, and then he turned to her with a smile.

"The old salts down here like to play a practical joke on greenhorns they find snooping around the boats. I thought I saw a guy who might do it, too. But don't take it too seriously. Can I give you a lift home?"

Jodi shook her head. "No, Mikkel is probably waiting for me at the car. Thanks for fishing me out of there, Mr. Burke!" He laughed and turned away, and she went back to the parking lot. Running over to the blue Volkswagen, she saw at once that Mikkel was not there!

The sun had disappeared behind a long, low mountain across the Cook Inlet, which Mr. Neilson had said was called Sleeping Lady, and the air was cool. She shivered and tried all the doors on the car. But they were locked, and her jacket was inside. Hugging herself, she tried to think. Where was Mikkel? Had something happened to her? Had someone pushed her into the hold so they could get Mikkel? The more she thought of it, the more convinced she became that someone had not been playing a practical joke.

But what should she do? Go back to the boat? She gazed at the quiet dock and canneries and took a deep breath. *Well, here goes! But this time I won't be caught!* Keeping well to the shadows, she crept back down the dock.

She was almost to the boat when she heard footsteps, and she ducked down behind some barrels. A tall, slim figure approached, and then passed. *The long-haired man again!* She waited until he had stepped into a cannery, and then she crept up to the boat and slipped quietly over the side.

Her heart was pounding in her ribs. Maybe she could go get the police. But she gritted her teeth to stop their chattering and crawled along the rough decking. Ahead she could see a sliver of light coming from a shaded window.

It was the cabin. Slowly she padded to the window and straightened up. Muffled voices came to her. Was that soft, musical one Mikkel's? Suddenly a door opened, and Jodi shrank back in the shadows and squeezed in behind a spool of netting.

The door shut, and two dark shadows thudded past her hiding place. Two men stepped off the boat and

58

disappeared down the dock. Jodi let out her breath. She waited several minutes, and when they did not return she slipped around the corner and found the door. She tried the doorknob, but it was locked.

Then, her heart pounding in her ears and her knees shaking, she put her mouth close to the crack and called out.

"Mikkel? Mikkel? Are you in there? This is Jodi." She heard a movement inside, and then Mikkel's voice answered her.

"Oh, Jodi! You found me! Get the police and hurry!"

Jodi shook her head. "There isn't time, Mikkel! I'll try to open this lock, but I don't have anything to work with! Do you have a bobby pin or a plastic card like a credit card?"

She heard some fumbling. "Here, Jodi," Mikkel answered. "It's coming under the door. A credit card."

Jodi grasped the card, slipped it between the lock and the doorjam, and worked it up and down. Footsteps on the dock caused her to pause and glance around the corner. The steps went on by.

Once again she set to work on the lock, and this time it opened! She flung back the door and Mikkel fell out. She was crying with relief, but Jodi grasped her arm and led her off the boat.

Again they slipped along the wooden planks, hiding in the shadows and holding their breath when someone came by. Then they were at the parking lot. They ran across it, but the little blue Volkswagen was gone!

Frantically they looked over the nearly vacant lot, but it was gone. On the ground Jodi found her jacket. She picked it up and shook it out, shaking her head.

"Well, at least I have my jacket," she said. "We have to get out of here and find a phone. Do you know where one is, Mikkel?"

Mikkel nodded. "I think so. Let's go!"

The friendly bright lights of a service station beckoned to them three blocks later. Jodi quickly entered the phone booth, took a dime from Mikkel, and put a call through to Mrs. Holmes. She sounded very relieved to hear Jodi's voice and promised she would be there soon.

"What did those men want of you?" Jodi asked Mikkel as they waited beside the phone booth.

Mikkel shook her head. "I just can't figure it out! They wanted to know where my father was, and where the painting I gave you was! You still have it, don't you?"

"No, I don't!" Jodi exclaimed. "That's what I came to talk to you about! It disappeared from the house today! Did you tell them I had it?"

Mikkel shook her head. "I wouldn't say anything."

"Did you recognize them? Who was that man with the pigtail?"

"I don't know his real name," Mikkel answered slowly, moving closer to the light. "They call him Loredo. I don't know who those other men were, either. They had handkerchiefs around their faces. But I did sort of recognize one voice. Just can't place it. What happened to you? You smell like a dead fish!"

Jodi shook her head. "I know. Someone grabbed me there on the boat and tossed me into the hold where they had fish. But listen, Mikkel. I think we should call the police and tell them what happened tonight! You're in danger!"

Mikkel's dark eyes flashed, and she grasped Jodi's arm.

"No! I won't call the police! Jodi, say you won't, either. Please? It—it's for my father. He was in jail a little while back, and it almost killed him. He's out on parole

60

now, and if he's caught mixed up in this mess somehow, and is in trouble—" She hesitated and Jodi saw a sparkle of tears in her eyes. "Please."

Jodi swallowed. What could she say? Maybe it wasn't really as bad as she had thought back there on the boat.

"Well, I'll promise for now, Mikkel," she said slowly, "but if you get caught again, or something else happens—"

"Oh, thanks, Jodi!" Mikkel flashed her a smile. A red station wagon pulled up beside the phone booth just then, and Jodi, followed by Mikkel, scrambled in.

Mrs. Holmes was shaking her head. "You've given us quite a scare, girls," she said, driving out into the street. "The Neilsons were about to call the police. Where have you been? And, Jodi! You smell awful!"

Jodi smiled a little. "I know. I had a little initiation on the docks tonight! Mikkel and I came down to see the cannery and fishing boats, and some guys pulled some tricks on us. Then Mikkel's friend took off with his car, so we had no way home."

It was ten minutes to seven when Jodi stepped into the Neilson's house, and everyone came into the kitchen. She stood awkwardly, shifting from one foot to another.

"I'm sorry I'm late," she said in a low voice. Mr. Neilson paced across the room, frowning.

"We've been very concerned about you, I must say that, Jodi," he said in a strained voice. "Do you have an explanation?"

Jodi swallowed a lump in her throat and sniffed. "Well, I went over to—"

"What is that horrid smell!" Mrs. Neilson interrupted, turning to look at Jodi from the sink. She grabbed a napkin and held it over her nose.

"It's her!" Stanley exclaimed, pointing at Jodi and

61

grinning. "She smells like a rotten fish!"

"I'll go clean up first, if you want," she said, turning as if to go, but Mr. Neilson shook his head.

"I would like to hear what you have to say," he said. "Right now, and without any further interruptions."

Jodi leaned against the breakfast bar. "I went over to see Mikkel this afternoon, and she invited me to go down to the docks with her. She was going to show me the canneries and fishing boats. We thought we would have lots of time to get back. But something happened—" She hesitated.

"Yes?" Mr. Neilson said, raising his eyebrows.

"Well, some guys down there played some tricks on us," she said. "They pushed me into the hold of a boat, and they locked Mikkel in the cabin. Then I got out and freed Mikkel, and her friend, whose car she was driving, took off with his car and left us stranded, so we had to walk to call home."

Stanley whistled. "Whew! That's a good one, Jodi!"

Mr. Neilson frowned at him and turned to Jodi. "You know you are welcome here in our home. But while you are with us, you have to understand that you must obey the rules of this house. We don't want to make it uncomfortable for you, but we are responsible for your actions, and we will not allow you to run around Anchorage at all hours of the night. You have to be home and dressed for dinner." He shook his head. "I trust nothing like this happens again, or else— " He let the sentence hang and turned to go into the living room.

"Can—can I go?" Jodi asked, tears stinging her eyes.

"Please!" Mrs. Neilson exclaimed.

Jodi fled from the room.

In the dark, on her bed, tears flooded her pillow. Finally she sat up, turned on the lamp, and began undressing. *How come I get blamed for everything,* she thought bitterly. *They don't really care about me! It was just their precious dinner I upset!*

But after her bath she felt better. She was combing out her wet hair when MaryAnn came in with a tray of food.

"Here." MaryAnn set the tray on the dresser and shook her head. "Aunt Phyllis fixed you some supper." By her tone, Jodi knew her friend was horribly embarrassed by the trouble she had caused.

"So they felt compassion on the delinquent?" Jodi asked angrily. "And I've shamed you again!"

MaryAnn sighed and sat down on her bed. "Well, really, Jodi! What do you expect? You're almost two hours late for dinner, and we're all worried and chewing our fingernails, and then you come in smelling like a—"

"—rotten fish," Jodi finished for her. Suddenly she began laughing, and MaryAnn grinned.

"OK, Jodi," she said. "Tell me the whole story. There's no one in the world who can get into trouble like you can! I guess I should learn to expect it, but you always surprise me!"

Jodi shook her head, got the tray, and sat down on her bed. She told MaryAnn all that had happened, while she ate roast turkey, mashed potatoes, gravy, and peas.

MaryAnn's brown eyes widened. "That doesn't sound like tricks to me! Someone is after that painting! We should call the police!"

"We can't," Jodi said, starting on the chocolate cake. "I promised Mikkel I wouldn't. She's afraid her father will be mixed up in it, and it will get him in trouble. Anyway, what would we say? We have nothing to go on."

"Nothing to go on!" MaryAnn repeated. "You get attacked, and Mikkel gets captured and threatened! I

63

don't care what you promised Mikkel, we should call the police!"

"Just give me some time," Jodi pleaded. "Look, MaryAnn. We're going out to the Evanses' soon, and I'll invite Mikkel to come along, and that will get her out of danger for a while."

MaryAnn nodded. "OK. We're going tomorrow, and I can't wait!" She glanced at the dresser. "But what I can't figure out is why those men want that painting!"

Jodi finished her milk and wiped her mouth with the napkin. Then she leaned back against the pillow and shook her head.

"I don't know," she said. "First it's stolen from the house, and then Mikkel gets captured and some men ask her where it is! Hey! There must be two groups who want it!"

"That's right." MaryAnn nodded. "And that Smith guy has something to do with all of this!"

Jodi sighed. "Well, tomorrow we're leaving Anchorage, and maybe we'll be leaving this mystery, too. We might never know the answers, MaryAnn!"

MaryAnn shook her head. "I wonder, Jodi," she said. "Mysteries have a way of following you around!"

The first thing next morning Jodi called Mikkel. The Eskimo girl seemed eager to get out of the city. As Jodi replaced the phone in the family room, she felt a warm gladness that for once she had helped someone. She went up for breakfast.

Mr. Neilson had gone to work, and Stanley was still sleeping, so Jodi and MaryAnn sat at the breakfast bar. Mrs. Neilson poured herself a cup of coffee and sat down with them.

She looked at MaryAnn. "So you're going to visit with the Evanses. I have a feeling you'll want to come back to the city soon. I really don't see how they can live out there in such a primitive fashion! Imagine! Going back to outhouses and wood stoves!"

MaryAnn and Jodi exchanged amused glances.

"Did you get hold of Mikkel?" MaryAnn asked Jodi.

Jodi nodded. "She said she'd love to get out of the city! I'm sure it would do her a lot of good, too. So we'll have to go over and pick her up before we go."

Mrs. Neilson's attitude had been cool to Jodi all morning, and now, ignoring her, she turned to MaryAnn.

"Mikkel?" she asked, raising her eyebrows.

MaryAnn nodded. "Yes. We thought it would be nice if she could come along, Aunt Phyllis. So Jodi called her this morning."

"But, my dear!" Mrs. Neilson said. "You should have asked me before you called! We can't take another guest out to the Evanses' without first checking with them! And I have no way of doing that!"

"But, Aunt Phyllis! They wouldn't mind. They're not like that. It doesn't matter if—"

"It certainly does, MaryAnn," Mrs. Neilson said in a voice that allowed for no differences of opinion. She strode to the sink. "And now you have this Eskimo girl all excited and ready to go! Well, you'll just have to call and tell her she can't go this time!"

Jodi felt her heart sink to her toes and her stomach tighten. Once again she had caused trouble! She blinked her long lashes against the tears.

"They—they have a CB radio, Mrs. Neilson," she said, her voice squeaky with tension. "Do you know anyone up that way you could call on the phone? Someone could pass the information on to them, surely."

Mrs. Neilson sighed wearily and glanced at her. "Well, there is a woman I know who does that sort of thing. I guess I could call her." She picked up the phone and a short time later replaced the receiver.

"She got through to them," she said, "and they said it was all right for her to come. Though why she would want to is beyond me! I'll finish straightening the kitchen. You girls get your things together. Howard will be at the lake soon."

Stanley stepped into the room, his brown hair disheveled.

"Can I come along, Mom?" he asked. "I missed going with them the other day."

Mrs. Neilson shook her head. "I'm afraid not this time, dear. Jodi invited Mikkel to go, so there won't be room."

Stanley whirled and followed Jodi and MaryAnn down the steps to their room.

"So our stupid little friend does it again!" He sneered. "How do you manage to cause so much trouble, dodo?"

Jodi was about to turn on him when MaryAnn grasped her arm tightly and pulled her into the bedroom, slamming the door behind them.

An hour later, Jodi was looking anxiously at the dark clouds overhead as Mr. Neilson loaded up the small blue and white plane at Hood Lake.

"Is it OK for flying?" she asked him nervously.

He glanced up. "The ceiling is still high. I just hope it doesn't drop before I get back. C'mon, what else do we have to load there?"

Jodi turned to grab another suitcase, and just then she saw something moving farther on down the shore. She looked up. It was a small, dark man slipping in behind Mr. Burke's plane! Her heart began thudding irregularly in her chest.

What was he doing? She glanced around and then ran

down to Mr. Burke's orange Super Cub. Popping around the side, she faced the man who stood there. *Mr. Smith!*

"So, it is you!" Jodi said, panting for breath. "Who are you, and what are you doing here?"

The Frenchman had been peering intently through the window of the small plane. Now he swung around, his fist flying! But with a look of surprise, he checked himself and turned to dash off.

Jodi jumped and caught his jacket. He paused long enough to wrench her fingers from it, and then he was gone, running like a frightened deer. She started to run after him.

"Jodi!" It was Mr. Neilson, and there was a note of irritation in his voice. She whirled and ran back to the others on the dock. Mrs. Neilson was frowning.

"There was a man sneaking around Mr. Burke's plane!" Jodi said, panting and pointing back. The man was gone. "Didn't you see him run off? I tried to stop him, but I couldn't."

Mr. Neilson looked over at the other plane and then shook his head. "Well, he's gone now, and if we don't get off, we won't be going today." He climbed into the pilot's seat, and Jodi, MaryAnn, and Mikkel followed him.

Jodi sat in the back next to Mikkel and fastened her seat belt as Mr. Neilson taxied out onto the lake and requested permission for take-off. She sighed when they were finally in the sky. She was glad to be leaving.

Mikkel touched her arm. "Jodi?" she asked, her voice raised above the roar of the motor. "Did you see that man?"

Jodi nodded, and brushed her fingers through her hair. "It was the man who followed us last night. That Mr. Smith. I think he might be the one who got the painting you gave me."

Mikkel's dark eyes widened, and she shook her head in dismay. "What was he doing?"

"Just looking in the window," Jodi replied. "Wish I could've caught him!"

She was left to her own thoughts the rest of the trip over the brown swirling rivers, the small settlements, and the seemingly endless muskeg with its marsh and stunted trees. Once she spotted the antlered brown form of a big moose feeding below.

Later they were circling Lucy Lake, and Jodi spotted the Evanses' dock. Two small figures waited on it, watching the plane's approach. They dipped down swiftly and then they were there, Jay tying the plane and helping MaryAnn out and Mr. Evans greeting them with a big smile.

Jodi introduced Mikkel to everyone. Mr. Neilson leaned over and called out to MaryAnn.

"I'll check with you in a few days," he said. "If anything happens, get in touch with us. Good-by!" Mr. Evans lifted out the suitcases and sleeping bags and pushed the plane away from the dock. They watched it lift off the water, and then waved as it circled and the wings dipped in a farewell salute. Then it was gone over the treetops.

"I'm glad you could make it," Mr. Evans said as he and Jay picked up the suitcases. "The looks of those clouds, I didn't know if Howard would bring you in or not."

Jodi smiled. "I'm glad, too. I was getting claustrophobia in that city! This is more my kind of living!"

"It's my kind of living, too!" Jay commented, his eyes on MaryAnn's slender form ahead of him. She laughed, her cheeks turning red.

Mrs. Evans greeted them in the warm kitchen with a

friendly hug. "Now, where would you girls like to stay? We have the tent pitched outside." She pointed out the kitchen door to a small, brightly colored orange tent pitched under the huge birch trees.

"And there's a bedroom in here, or the couch," she continued. "MaryAnn?"

MaryAnn glanced around. "Oh, I'm not much of a camper. I'd rather stay in here."

Mrs. Evans nodded and looked at Jodi.

She looked out at the tent. "I think I'd like to sleep out there," she said, "Just so long as it doesn't rain."

Mikkel nodded. "I'll go with Jodi," she said softly.

Mrs. Evans smiled. "OK. Jay can sleep on the couch, and MaryAnn can have his bedroom. The other two girls can sleep in the tent."

Soon after Jodi and Mikkel had their sleeping bags and belongings settled in the tent, Jodi slipped down the path to the outhouse. The stillness of the wilderness brought peace to her ragged nerves and troubled mind.

She breathed deeply of the woodsy air and listened to the sounds. High in the branches of the tall trees, the wind sighed, and lower down the thick bushes rustled. She heard the patter of some small animal scurrying off in the underbrush, and the chatter of a squirrel high in a tree.

But there was something else—something big moving cautiously through the woods nearby! Was it a moose? A bear? She froze to the spot, her heart pounding and her eyes straining to see through the thick curtain of green bushes and undergrowth.

And then she saw the head and shoulders of a man slowly working his way through the bushes! His face was turned away, but then, as if sensing her eyes upon him, he turned.

Jodi caught a glimpse of dark hair and black, flashing eyes, and then he was gone.

6

The Strange Red Beaver

Jodi felt a scream rising in her throat. She covered her mouth with her hand and ran to the cabin.

"Mrs. Evans!" she burst out. "There was a man right over there in the bushes!" Mrs. Evans turned from the stove and looked at her in shocked surprise.

"A man! Walter!"

Mr. Evans appeared in the kitchen and heard Jodi's announcement. He and Jay tramped outside. Jodi watched them going through the woods behind the cabin. Several minutes later they returned.

"Nothing out there now," Mr. Evans said, frowning. "I can't imagine who it would be, unless it was just someone hiking around."

"Do you still want to stay in the tent, Jodi?" Mrs. Evans asked.

"I'm all right," Jodi said. She glanced at Mikkel, who was standing very still, her eyes wide and her face pale. "Mikkel? How about you?"

She seemed to shake herself. "I'm OK."

"I'd like to look outside some more," Jodi said, going to the door. "Maybe he dropped something." Jay and MaryAnn followed her out, but they went down to the dock.

Jodi stooped over and studied the soft, mossy ground,

pushing the bushes aside. After looking around for some time, she straightened up with a sigh.

"I guess there's nothing out here after all," she said to herself. "Hey, there's something!" She picked up a book of matches and turned it over. There were words scribbled on the back.

"Evans. Lucy Lake," she read. "That guy must have dropped this!"

She rushed down to the dock where Jay and MaryAnn were talking. "Look! I found this on the ground where that man was!" she exclaimed, handing Jay the matches.

The breeze lifted his golden brown hair from his forehead as he took the matches and MaryAnn crowded close.

"It doesn't prove much, though," he said, handing them back to Jodi. "Except that he knows our name and he smokes." Then he grinned. "Pretty good detective work, though, Sherlock!"

Jodi laughed and met his hazel eyes. "I'll keep these, anyway. It may be a good clue later on."

"The great girl detective does it again!" MaryAnn said dramatically, giving Jodi a short bow.

Jay turned to her and laughed. "Well, maybe she can figure out who threw you into the lake, beautiful!" He grasped her shoulders and pushed her toward the edge of the dock. She shrieked and involuntarily reached for him.

Jodi turned away. "Can't you guys be serious? Man, we have a mystery and all you can do is—" She gestured with a sweep of her arm and glanced at them.

"Poor Jodi." MaryAnn laughed. "I think she misses her boyfriend, Stanley!"

"Stanley!" Jay picked up the teasing and gave her a shove. "Jodi and Stanley! Jodi's got a boyfriend!"

72

Seething with anger, she sprang off the dock. "Drop dead, you guys!" she heard herself yelling. "MaryAnn, you think you're so smart. Well, you're not!" She stomped up the hill, hearing Jay and MaryAnn laughing as she went.

That night, Jodi fought down a queasy feeling in her stomach and followed Mikkel out to the tent. The woods that were so friendly and peaceful that morning were full of shadows and rustling noises now. She hurriedly undressed and crawled into her sleeping bag.

Mikkel scrambled into hers. "What did that man look like, Jodi?" she asked, peering over the sleeping bag.

Jodi frowned. "Let's not talk about it, Mikkel," she said.

"No, Jodi, I want to know," Mikkel persisted. Her round face, framed with her dark hair, bent toward Jodi. Her black, slanting eyes were wide and staring.

"I—I can't really remember," Jodi stammered. "It was gone so fast. But he had dark hair and eyes. I was thinking it was Mr. Smith, but I don't think it was now."

"Why not?"

Jodi pondered that for a moment. "Well, in the flash that I saw his face, I had the impression it was fatter, and older, too. I don't know, Mikkel. I found a book of matches he dropped. Here, I'll show you."

She sat up and dug in the pocket of her jeans for a moment. Then she handed the book of matches to Mikkel. Mikkel's eyes widened, and she drew in her breath sharply. Jodi looked at her.

"What is it? Do you know who this belongs to?"

Mikkel gazed at the matchbook for a long time, turning it over in her hand. When she looked up, her face and eyes were blank.

"No, I guess not," she said in a low voice, handing

73

them back to Jodi. "I thought I recognized the writing, but I guess I was wrong." She lay down. "Good night."

Jodi put the matches in her suitcase and lay down, puzzled at Mikkel's answer. She was sure she had seen recognition in Mikkel's eyes. What was she hiding from her? Why wouldn't she say? Finally Jodi rolled over and dropped off to sleep.

Mikkel was gone when she opened her eyes the next morning, and for a few seconds she couldn't remember where she was. There was a dull orange light all around. Then she knew! She sat up. The orange light was from the sun shining through the tent. *What day is it?* she wondered, rubbing her eyes. *Oh, Friday! Only ten more days in Alaska, and I'm going to make the most of them!* She thought about Jay dreamily. *If only I could have him all to myself.*

Suddenly someone approached the tent and rattled the side. "Come on!" MaryAnn called cheerfully. "Waffles are on!"

"Waffles!" Jodi jumped up, threw on her clothes, and shrugged on her jacket. Mornings were chilly in Alaska, even in the summer. After brushing her hair, she patted down her sleeping bag and dashed to the cabin.

Mrs. Evans looked up from the wood stove. Her cheeks were rosy from the heat, and a strand of gray hair straggled across her forehead, but she smiled cheerfully and motioned to the table.

"This one is for you, Jodi," she said. "Come and sit down, before Mr. Evans and Jay eat them all!" She turned over the old-fashioned waffle iron above the fire.

Jodi poured some warm water from the stove into a basin at the sink and washed her hands and face. Then she sat down.

"Sorry I'm late," she said.

Mr. Evans chuckled. "You would have been if I'd eaten all the waffles!"

After breakfast, Jodi and MaryAnn cleaned up the kitchen.

Jay lingered near MaryAnn. "Listen, doll," he said, drooping his arm around her shoulders. "Let's go fishing. I know where we can catch some big ones!"

MaryAnn slipped out from under his arm. "Fishing isn't my thing, Jay," she said, blushing.

"OK, then, let's go for a walk," Jay replied, lacing up his boots. "I know some good places around here. We might even spot some wildlife. Come on!"

MaryAnn, pulled along by Jay, grabbed her jacket and went out the door with him. Jodi watched as they disappeared down the trail, hand in hand. She frowned.

"Oh, that Jay makes me sick! We ought to follow them and spoil their fun!"

Mrs. Evans came into the kitchen. "I just hope he isn't a bad influence on MaryAnn. He's a Christian, but he's not living for the Lord right now."

Jodi nodded soberly, suddenly embarrassed as she realized Mrs. Evans had overheard her outburst. Why couldn't she control her tongue? Sometimes she wished she could bite it off!

She sighed. "Well, I guess we could go fishing, Mikkel," she said. "How about it?"

Mikkel was finishing the drying job MaryAnn had left. She shook her head. "I'd rather not," she said softly.

"Why not take the boat out by yourself?" Mrs. Evans suggested, patting Jodi's arm. "You know how to run an outboard motor, don't you? OK. Remember to put on a life jacket, dear."

Jodi found the life jackets in a small shed beside the dock down at the lake. Flinging one on and tying it, she got into a small green boat and pulled the cord on the outboard motor. Soon she was putt-putting across the lake.

She lifted her face to the cool breeze that blew her hair back. In the distance she could see Mount McKinley jutting up white and big against the blue sky. Ducks lifted up from the lake as she approached, quacking their disapproval.

It was a beautiful, still morning with white, puffy clouds reflected in the greenish blue water and the boat cleaving a path of wrinkles in the smooth surface. The lake had many fingers of land jutting out, creating dozens of interesting little coves. Up ahead, Jodi saw the first of several little islands that dotted the lake.

Here and there, set back among the trees, she caught sight of several cabins. She rounded a peninsula that had a tall, jagged snag at the top. On the far side, she saw a large cabin and several boats tied to the dock. An older man was standing on the dock, watching her.

She waved, but he just stared. With a jolt, she realized the long thing under his arm was a gun! Abruptly she steered the boat toward a small island out in the lake.

Jodi cut the motor as she approached the shore. She hopped out and pulled the boat up higher on the grassy slope. Then she spent the better part of an hour exploring the island, sinking in past her ankles in the soft, springy tundra, and looking for wildflowers. She found wild roses in bloom, the blue lupine, a tiny white flower that grew in the moss, and some bright red fireweed.

"Well! There are flowers out here!" she said to herself with a smile. Suddenly she heard a motor. Returning to the boat, she looked out over the water, but there was nothing coming across the lake. The motor was louder now, and she looked up. It was a plane coming in.

Was it MaryAnn's uncle coming to check on them? No, she could see it was much bigger than Mr. Neilson's Cessna. The plane was red, and it taxied quite close to where she was standing. Suddenly her pulse quickened. Mr. Evans had said he had seen a strange red plane on the lake! Maybe this was the gang of thieves!

There were numbers on the side of the plane, and she said them aloud. "P-four seven three two. P-forty-seven thirty-two." And then she saw the passenger on her side—it was a man with long, dark hair caught back in a pigtail—the man Mikkel called Loredo!

With goosebumps on her arms, she watched as the plane taxied up to the dock where she had seen the old man. The passenger got out, the plane was turned around, and then it took off with a roar over her head. The old man and Loredo met on the dock and then went up the hill to the cabin.

Her heart pounding in her ears, she jumped into the boat and yanked on the starter cord. The motor leaped to life, and she headed for home. *Just wait till Jay hears about this!* she thought. *He'll forget all about MaryAnn and come out in the boat with me to spy on Loredo!*

At the Evanses' dock, she jumped out and began tying up the boat.

"Move that boat around!" Mr. Evans bellowed from up above her. Surprised, Jodi glanced up and saw him running down the hill. She jumped up and moved the boat around.

"What's the matter?" she asked as he came out on the dock and tied the boat for her.

"There's been an accident," he said as he straightened. His face was white. "MaryAnn cut her finger almost off!"

"Cut her—" she gulped, and then felt as if everything

77

was spinning. Mr. Evans grasped her arm tightly, and she blinked against the tears that were springing to her blue eyes.

"How—how did it happen?" she choked out.

He cleared his throat and glanced at the sky. "She was helping fix lunch, and she was cutting with a real sharp knife. It slipped and nearly went through her little finger! We've called in the air ambulance. Listen! That's them now! Jodi, you go on up and help with MaryAnn. I'll meet the plane."

Jodi ran up the hill and passed Jay coming down. "Is that the plane?" he asked. His face was pale.

Jodi nodded and ran on into the cabin. MaryAnn was lying on the couch in the living room. A quilt was covering her, and several pillows were under her feet. Her eyes were closed, and her face was chalky white. Her hand rested on her stomach and her little finger was bandaged with white strips of cloth.

"Oh, it's you, dear," Mrs. Evans said. "Come and sit by her. I'll get her things together."

Mikkel brought in her sleeping bag, "I've rolled this up," she said. Mrs. Evans thanked her and went to gather the rest of her things. Jodi knelt by MaryAnn and touched her cheek.

"MaryAnn?" she said softly. MaryAnn's eyes fluttered open. "The plane is here. You'll soon be in Anchorage."

MaryAnn turned her head and moaned. "It hurts so bad, Jodi!" she said. "But I don't want to go! I was having such a good time!"

Jodi patted her shoulder. "You'll be able to come back. Don't worry about it!"

Mr. Evans brought in two ambulance attendants. Jodi stepped aside as they carried MaryAnn out of the cabin, down the hill, and loaded her on the plane. Mrs. Evans shoved in MaryAnn's things, and Jay squeezed her good hand in farewell. Then they all stood wordlessly on the dock as the plane taxied out into the lake and took off with a roar.

Mrs. Evans leaned on her husband, crying quietly. "Oh, Walter! Let's pray!" Silently they all joined hands, even Mikkel, who hung back until Mrs. Evans pulled her into their circle. Mr. Evans led in a simple, earnest prayer for MaryAnn's recovery.

When Jodi looked up, she realized it was Jay who held her hand. He looked up at the same moment, and for several heartbeats she was looking into his hazel eyes. Then she pulled her hand away and started up to the cabin.

She helped Mrs. Evans put on lunch, and they all sat down, but no one was very hungry. Afterward, Jodi ran down to the dock and sat alone. A breeze was ruffling the lake into waves, and a cloud had covered the sun. She rubbed her arms and shivered. Poor MaryAnn! What a way to spend her holiday!

She heard footsteps and glanced up. It was Jay. His eyes were somber, and he didn't look at her as he sat down beside her on the dock. She looked at his dirty tennis shoes. He leaned his tanned arms on his knees and sighed, gazing out over the water. There was silence for what seemed like a long time as the waves slapped against the dock.

Finally he sighed again. "It's too bad," he said, glancing at her. "But it never would have happened if she hadn't wanted to come back from our walk!"

Jodi glanced at him sharply. "You sound like Stanley—never happy unless someone gets blamed!"

"So it's Stanley again, is it?" he retorted quickly. "Your boyfriend?"

79

She moved to the other side of the dock. A family of ducks swam quite near. Usually she would have laughed at the row of fluffy yellow ducklings and the clucking and quacking of the mother duck, but now she watched them dully.

Jay stood up. "Well, I'm not going to sit around and mope," he said. "Want to come with me for a ride in the big boat?"

She looked at him. Was he baiting her? Was he flirting just so he could laugh at her later? But he climbed in the boat and started up the powerful motor without another glance in her direction.

"Coming?" he asked finally.

She shrugged. "OK." Grabbing a life jacket, she jumped down on the seat beside him. *It's funny,* she thought, *a little while ago, I would have been in heaven if he had invited me for a boat ride! Now I'd give anything if MaryAnn were sitting here, not me!*

Jay crammed the throttle forward and turned the wheel. The boat lifted its prow out of the water and shot out into the lake. The wind took Jodi's breath away, but she loved it. They skimmed over the water as Jay skillfully steered around the islands and in and out of the coves.

After a little while, he slowed down and turned to her. "What's the matter, Jodi?" he asked. "You aren't enjoying this."

She studied him seriously. "How *can* I? After what happened to MaryAnn? And I don't know about you. I don't think I can trust you."

He shook his head. "Look. What's happened to MaryAnn has happened. We can't change it by dragging our heels. It's done. Right? So now we can have fun. OK?" He suddenly was laughing, his hazel eyes flecked with golden lights. He patted her shoulder. "You can trust me, Jodi. How about it?"

She hesitated and then grinned at him. "All right," she said. "Nothing like playing second fiddle, though!"

He laughed again and pushed the throttle forward. They rounded a finger of land, and Jodi saw a red plane straight ahead. Jay spotted it at the same moment and cut the motor.

"Hey, it's the same plane I saw earlier!" Jodi exclaimed. "It came in when I was out in the boat to the cabin over there. Whose place is that, anyway?"

Jay cut the motor and gazed at the plane, which was idling not too far from the beach.

"Oh, that's Mr. Adams's cabin," he said finally. "He's a real weirdo. No one ever goes there. He packs around a gun, and he has two mean dogs."

Jodi frowned. "I wonder why he's like that."

"I've wondered, too," Jay replied. "I wouldn't be surprised if he was a crook. And that's the red Beaver that Dad saw around here before! Let's try to get up to it!"

He shoved the throttle open, but the men in the plane must have been watching them. They gunned the motor on the plane, and soon it was skimming away. Jay followed it until it zoomed up and away, and then he turned the boat toward home. As they passed Mr. Adams's cabin, Jodi spotted the old man on the dock.

"There he is now," Jay said.

She nodded. "Maybe he knows about the red plane, Jay. Let's stop and ask!"

He hesitated. "He's not very friendly," he said, but he steered the boat across the cove. As they approached, Jodi could see he was frowning and cradling a gun in his arm.

"Hi, Mr. Adams!" Jay called out as he shut off the

motor and drifted up to the dock. But the old man's frown deepened. He was unshaven and dumpy, his gray hair straggling down around his face.

He spit on the dock near their boat. "Whaddya want?" he growled.

"There was a strange red Beaver in here just a little while ago," Jay began, "and we were wondering if you know who it belongs to and what they were doing."

The old man shifted his gun. "It ain't none of your business, boy. Just clear out, ya hear?"

"But, Mr. Adams," Jodi spoke up. "It may be the thieves! What is it doing out here?"

Mr. Adams' face turned red, and he lifted the gun so that it pointed at them.

Jodi shrank back.

"Git out of here, I said!" he yelled. "I don't want to say it twice!"

Jay turned the key, and the motor leaped to life. He wrenched the steering wheel around and soon they were racing back home.

At their dock, Jodi shook her head. "Wow! What a character! I bet he's in with the gang of crooks!" She took off her life jacket and hung it in the shed.

Jay hung his over hers. "He's a no-good creep!" He shook his head. "Let's go tell Dad."

Mr. Evans nodded when they described the red plane to him. "That was the same one I saw," he said. "I called the numbers in, and they said there wasn't any plane registered under them!" He shook his head. "I don't know what to do. The police wouldn't come out here unless we could prove something. And just because Mr. Adams is unfriendly doesn't mean he's in with the thieves. We'll just have to keep our eyes open and wait."

That night, Jodi snuggled down in her sleeping bag

and thought about Jay. *He's OK,* she decided. *Kind of crazy, but OK.* She rolled over and saw the back of Mikkel's head. She sighed. Quiet, unassuming Mikkel. And lately, she seemed even more quiet. What was bothering her? Was she afraid? Was she hiding something?

Jodi shut her eyes and tried to pray, but Jay's teasing, laughing eyes came into her mind. Finally she rolled over and went to sleep.

Sometime in the night, she awoke. It was very dark, so she knew it must be late. Her eyes fluttered shut again, and then she felt a movement in the tent! Someone was quietly crawling around beside her! She held her breath and slowly lifted her head.

7

A Meeting in the Dark

It was Mikkel! Jodi caught a glimpse of her jeans and tennis shoes as she disappeared through the tent door. She sat up. Where would she be going in the middle of the night?

Then she heard something wooden bumping. Oh—the outhouse! She was about to lie down when she heard the noise again. It was coming from the dock, and it sounded like an oar bumping on the side of a boat! In a flash she remembered seeing Mikkel's jeans and shoes. She was dressed and going somewhere in the dark!

Her fingers shaking, she pulled on her shoes, threw on her jacket, grabbed her flashlight, and stumbled from the tent. Padding softly down to the lake without using her flashlight, she peered out over the water. A boat was out there, being swiftly and silently rowed away.

"Mikkel!" she called, cupping her hands around her mouth. "Mikkel!" But her voice was lost out over the water and there was no reply. Jodi turned on her flashlight as she made her way up the hill to the tent.

Inside, she crawled in her sleeping bag and wondered what she should do. Should she go and get Mr. Evans? Was Mikkel running away? Finally she decided to wait for her to come back and then ask her where she had gone.

Long before Mikkel returned, Jodi's eyes closed in sleep. But it was a light sleep, and as the dawn began brightening up the sky, she felt a movement beside her and her eyes flew open.

Mikkel was just getting into her sleeping bag. Jodi sat up. "Mikkel! Where did you go?" she asked.

"Just for a ride," Mikkel said, yawning. She lay down and closed her eyes.

"Mikkel," Jodi repeated. "Where did you go? I know you wouldn't go out in the boat in the middle of the night unless you had a good reason."

Mikkel remained still, but finally she opened her eyes. "I think that's my business. Look, I'd like to get some sleep." She rolled over and pulled up her sleeping bag.

"Mikkel! I want to know where you went and why!" Jodi demanded. But the dark-haired girl was silent. Suddenly Jodi was hot and angry, and she spoke without thinking.

"I thought you wanted me to help you!" she stormed at Mikkel's back. "How can I help you if you won't tell me what's going on? Well, I don't care! You can just help yourself from now on! I should have known better than to try to help a stupid Eskimo!"

The moment the words were out, she was sorry she had said them. But she was too angry to admit it. She flopped down in her sleeping bag and pulled it up over her head.

Sometime much later she dozed off. But she was awakened soon after by a rustling beside her. Mikkel was getting up. Jodi lay still with her head covered by the sleeping bag. She tried to get back to sleep, but her conscience was screaming at her.

Finally she opened her eyes. She could just see the corner of her suitcase, and she knew that inside lay her

Bible—her Bible that she had not even opened this whole trip! But she didn't need to open it to know what it said.

Be ye kind one to another was one verse she had memorized as a child, and now it came back to her. Her angry, hateful words echoed in her mind, and she squeezed her eyes shut and bit her tongue until it hurt. Why couldn't she learn to think before she spoke? Why must she always hurt and destroy with this tongue?

"Lord, I'm sorry," she whispered. "I'm sorry I said that to Mikkel. Please forgive me and wash me clean. Help me to be a good friend to her. In Jesus' name. Amen."

Slowly she crawled out of bed, still feeling sick inside. She knew she would have to apologize, but she didn't know how she would do it.

The family was seated at the table when she came into the cabin, and Mrs. Evans was frying eggs. Mikkel was making toast in the oven. The heat from the stove felt good. Mrs. Evans placed a platter of bacon and eggs on the table, and Mikkel plunked down the plate of toast. She sat down and stared at her plate as they said the blessing.

"Good morning, Jodi," Mr. Evans said. "We heard from the Neilsons this morning. Kind of bad news for you, I'm afraid. They called MaryAnn's parents, and they want you both to come home right away. They've booked a flight for you for tomorrow night, and Mr. Neilson is coming for you this afternoon."

Jodi started up and choked on her juice. When she had recovered, she looked at Mr. Evans with her big blue eyes.

"Why! Isn't her injury healing?"

Mr. Evans shook his head. "They didn't say."

Jodi stared at the food on her plate and felt tears

gathering in her eyes. "But I don't want to go home!" she said. "Couldn't I stay and fly home alone?"

"I know it's hard, dear," Mrs. Evans said, putting her hand on her shoulder. "But these things do come up, and we just have to make the best of them. You should plan on flying home with MaryAnn as that seems to be what the Neilsons want."

Jodi sighed and shook her head. "I suppose Stanley is to be thanked for that!" she muttered. Then she turned to Mr. Evans.

"Couldn't I stay out here until tomorrow afternoon? There's nothing for me to do in the city."

"Well, we'd love to have you," Mr. Evans said. "But—"

Jodi held her breath. Oh, how she wanted to stay!

"I don't see why she and Mikkel couldn't stay," Mrs. Evans put in, pouring the coffee. "Mr. Neilson could come out for them Sunday afternoon."

Mr. Evans shook his head. "That's cutting it too close," he said around a mouthful of toast. "What if the ceiling drops and a plane couldn't come in?"

Jodi laid her fork down. "I'll get out in time. If it looks bad, he could come right away. Please?"

Mr. Evans smiled. "OK. I guess we could always go across the lake and drive in. I'll have to get in touch with the Neilsons."

"All right!" Jay said softly and flashed Jodi a grin. She smiled back, but then her spirits dropped as she glanced at Mikkel. Mikkel got up from the table and went to the living room. She had not said a word.

"Something is troubling that girl," Mrs. Evans said in a low voice. "Have you any idea what it is, Jodi?"

Jodi sighed. "Lots. Her father left her, and she's pretty lonely. And last night she left the tent, and I got mad when she wouldn't tell me where she had gone. I—I guess I should go apologize, but I don't know—"

Mrs. Evans nodded. "You go, Jodi," she said. "I'll pray."

Jodi went to the living room where Mikkel was leafing through a magazine and sat down on the couch beside her. Her heart was thumping and her mouth was dry.

"Mikkel?" she said softly. Mikkel didn't look up and only turned the pages more rapidly. Jodi swallowed.

"I—I just wanted to say I'm sorry for what I said last night," she said.

Mikkel finished the magazine, flopped it down, and picked up another one without a glance at Jodi.

"I was wrong to pry into your affairs, and I'm always saying things I don't mean. I'd still like to be your friend, Mikkel." The last word died on her lips, and her throat constricted as tears flooded her eyes. Mikkel had given no indication that she had even heard her.

Jodi sprang up and went back to the kitchen. Mrs. Evans raised her eyebrows. Jodi shook her head and dashed out the door, stumbling down to the dock. At the dock, she watched the waves lapping against the sides of the boats.

It was overcast and chilly—a day that matched her mood. Here she was going home tomorrow night and she hadn't tried to solve Mikkel's mystery, or the mystery of the thieves at the lake! Maybe the best way to prove her sincerity to Mikkel would be to really help her. But where could she start?

Jay came down to the dock, carrying several empty five-gallon water containers.

"Why so low?" He laughed, tousling her curly hair. "Let's go get some drinking water."

She frowned and tried to smooth down her hair. "OK, but you gotta promise to be nice!" He laughed again,

88

and she ran up the hill for her jacket. In the tent, she paused. Mikkel's jean jacket lay thrown across her sleeping bag.

Jodi leaned over and picked it up. Would there be a clue as to where she went last night? She looked it over, and then on the sleeve she saw several burrs stuck to the material.

"So she went into the woods!" she exclaimed, removing one of the burrs. Suddenly she thought of the book of matches—her other clue—and bent down to get it out of her suitcase.

But she couldn't find it! She took nearly everything out and shook her clothes, but it was gone! She straightened up, frowning. *Mikkel must have taken it,* she thought. *But why?*

She made her way thoughtfully down to the dock and while she and Jay put on their life jackets, she told him about Mikkel's secret trip in the night and the book of matches. She showed him the burr from Mikkel's jacket. She also told him about Loredo and how she had seen him coming in on the red Beaver.

Jay frowned. "Hm. Sneaking off at night. Maybe she's in with the thieves! And taking that book of matches—"

"I can't figure it out!" Jodi exclaimed.

"Hey, I wonder if she's going out again tonight," he replied, snapping his fingers. "Because if she is, I know where we can get a canoe, and we'll follow her!" He got in the boat and Jodi followed him.

"Follow her?" she asked.

He laughed. "You'll see." The boat shot out of the water. The ride down and back was exciting, and by the time they got back, Jodi's spirits were lifted. It was raining lightly as they pulled up by the dock and Mr. Evans met them. He hefted out the water cans.

"Doesn't look so good," he said to Jodi. "I got hold of Mr. Neilson, but I'm not so sure about it now. It could really sock in by tomorrow."

"Oh, Dad, the ceiling is still high," Jay countered. Jodi picked up a water can and lugged it up the hill, thinking her arms were going to fall off before she got to the cabin. Jay carried two with ease, and Jodi suddenly knew how he got such strong arms!

After lunch, Jay went outside in the rain, and Jodi helped Mrs. Evans can some fresh salmon she had been given. Later she wandered outside and down to the dock. The rain had let up, and she smiled to see a patch of blue sky showing through the clouds. But where was Jay?

Suddenly he appeared out of the bushes, grinning. "C'mere, Jodi." He beckoned mysteriously. Jodi ran over to where he was, and taking her hand he led her down a trail by the lake. Breaking out on the beach, he pointed to a canoe.

"Where did you get it?" Jodi asked a little breathlessly, terribly aware of how tightly he held her hand.

His hazel eyes twinkled. "Borrowed it. Some people live down the lake a ways. Friends of ours, the Peterses." He motioned vaguely down the lake.

"Will they mind? Don't you think we should tell your father?" She led the way back to the dock and sat down.

"Are you nuts?" he exclaimed sharply. "Listen, it's gotta be just between you and me!" He sat down beside her and put his arm around her shoulders. "OK, sweetheart?" he said in her ear. She caught a whiff of something as he put his face close to hers. Was it aftershave? Suddenly she shoved him away and ran up the hill to the cabin.

That night, Jodi's mind was filled with doubts. What if Mikkel didn't go out? What if they got caught? Was it right to spy on the girl she was trying to befriend and help?

Once again, a strong sickening feeling of guilt flooded over her. Mikkel was struggling alone with problems so overwhelming that Jodi could only guess at how she felt. And yet what had she done to help? She had blown everything in one careless outburst!

Tears trickled down her cheek, and she wiped them off. How she longed to reach across the gap that had widened between them and help this shy, sensitive girl! Sighing, she rolled over and wondered if she would be able to stay awake. Sleep was tugging at her eyes, and her long lashes drooped. Suddenly she was wide awake! Mikkel was slowly moving beside her!

Jodi lay still while Mikkel slipped noiselessly out of the tent. After she was gone, Jodi sat up. Her heart pounding in her ears, she slipped on her shoes. Picking up her flashlight, she stepped out in the dark.

At last they would find out where Mikkel had been going! Quickly she made her way to Jay's window and tossed a small stone at it. Then she followed the trail down the hill.

In the dim light she could see the small green boat was gone. They would have to hurry if they were going to follow Mikkel! She heard a movement behind her, and a few seconds later Jay took her hand and led the way to where he had beached the canoe.

Jodi's pulse pounded and her breath was rapid. This was exciting! Slipping out in the middle of the night to follow someone with a big, tall, handsome boy who held her hand tightly in his! And maybe they would solve the mystery of the thieves on the lake!

Silently they climbed in the canoe and paddled out into the lake. Jodi strained her eyes and ears.

"Over that way!" Jay whispered, pointing down the lake. "I heard an oar bumping on the boat. Let's go!"

They paddled swiftly and quietly toward the sounds, and then Jodi made out a dark shadow ahead on the water. They rested for a few seconds and then followed slowly.

A little later, Jodi leaned back. "Where are we?"

He put his face near hers. "Over that point of land is Adams's place. She must be going to meet that man—her friend with the long hair."

"Could be," Jodi replied, nodding.

He laid his hand on her shoulder and pulled her closer. She felt his breath on her cheek, and she jerked away from him and began paddling. Her heart was thumping madly. Peering ahead into the darkness, she could not see Mikkel's boat. They had lost it!

"Where did she go?" she whispered without turning back.

He was studying the shore. "I think she beached the boat along the shore over there," he said. "She's probably meeting him somewhere in the woods."

"There it is!" Jodi said as they approached the beach. She hopped out as Jay ran the canoe up on the beach, and then he joined her. A small animal trail led into the bushes. Jodi handed her flashlight to Jay.

"You go first," she whispered.

He wrapped his arms around her. "What's the hurry, Jodi?" he whispered in her ear. "Let's enjoy the moment!"

She pushed him away violently. "Stop it! You don't even care about Mikkel, do you!" Suddenly she saw him for what he was—a self-centered flirt. She turned away from him in disgust.

"Sure I care!" he replied coolly. "I care enough to see her caught! Come on!"

He started up the trail, stepping lightly over the sticks and pushing his way through the bushes. He didn't stop to look back at her as she followed as best as she could. Once she stumbled and by the time she had regained her feet, she was alone.

She tried to still her thumping heart and noisy breathing to listen. There! Over to the side and up the hill was the sound of something moving through the bushes. She started toward the sounds. The woods were dark, and she began wishing she had stayed home when she saw a dusky light ahead. Just then Jay's hand gripped her arm. She jumped and nearly yelled, but his other hand covered her mouth.

"Look!" he whispered in her ear. "Over there!" Peering out through the fringe of bushes, she saw two shadowy figures huddled together near a large stump.

"We'll go closer," Jay whispered again. "You sound like an elephant! Be quiet and follow me!"

She made a face at his back and followed close behind him as he wormed his way closer to the two shadows. Her heart was pounding and her breath came in gasps.

Was it Mikkel and Loredo? Was Mikkel really involved with a gang of crooks? Suddenly she didn't want to know. She yanked on Jay's arm, and he turned to her.

"Let's go home!" she urged. "This isn't right!"

He shook his head. "No way! I'm going to see what's going on! Come on, now!"

Finally they stopped, and they could overhear the low conversation. Jodi heard Mikkel's soft voice.

"Listen to me!" Her words were urgent and insistent. "You'll spend your whole life running! You can't do that! I need you. There's only one thing you can do. Please—"

A low, gutteral voice interrupted her. "*Paniga.** I hear what you are saying. But what will become of you? It is for you that I run. I am spying on them, and I will find out something—" He sighed. "But these men, they do not know kindness. Mikkel, for you I must run and hide!"

Mikkel was crying softly on his shoulder, shaking her head, and saying something so low Jodi could not hear. She let out her breath. So it wasn't Loredo! It was her father!

Mikkel's voice went on—urging, pleading, begging. Tears came to Jodi's eyes, and she knew they had no right to be there, eavesdropping on a very private conversation. She turned to Jay and pulled on his sleeve.

"I'm going, Jay," she mouthed, motioning with her hand back toward the lake. "We shouldn't be here. Come on."

He shook his head violently and turned to look again at Mikkel and her father. Jodi pulled angrily on his arm, rising from her crouched position at the same time. But he shook her away, and suddenly she felt herself falling.

She tried to get her feet underneath her, but her toes caught on a root and she threw out her arms, trying to grab Jay.

But it was no use. With a loud splintering crash, she fell heavily out of the bushes, almost at the feet of Mikkel and her father. And as she landed, she heard a man's loud guttural shout and a girl's scream.

---

*Paniga—daughter.

8

The Words of My Mouth

When Jodi looked up, dazed, Mikkel was alone. The scream had died on her lips, and she was staring at Jodi in stunned surprise. Jodi unscrambled herself from the bushes and stood up.

"It's me, Mikkel," she said sheepishly. "I—I'm sorry. I—"

"You followed me!" Mikkel was trembling with rage. "You—you dirty rat! You spoiled everything! Do you hear me? Everything!" Tears began rolling down her round cheeks, and she whirled away from Jodi and covered her face with her hands.

"My father—he was going to come with me—but you scared him away—and now he's running again!" She turned on Jodi, and now her voice was low and quivering.

"I don't ever want to see you again, Jodi Fischer! I'm leaving this place. Now! And don't bother looking for me! Just stay out of my life!" And then she ran off into the woods.

Jodi jumped after her, tears stinging her eyes. "No, wait! Mikkel! Please!" She followed her a short way into the thick underbrush and then stopped. Where was Jay? Which way did he go? Where was Mikkel? She listened and heard twigs breaking a short distance away in the woods.

"Jay?" she called, hurrying toward the sounds. But it was not Jay, and when she stopped to listen again, the woods were silent. Looking around fearfully, she shivered and tried to decide which way to go. Jay still had her flashlight!

If that wasn't Jay, what was it? she wondered. *An animal? Mikkel's father?* She listened for some time and then sighed.

"Well, I heard noises in that direction, so I'll go that way," she said to herself. "But it doesn't seem right." Slowly she picked her way through the bushes, over logs, and always downhill. Eventually she had to come out at the lake, and then she could find the boat. Mikkel's words came back to her and she paused in the darkness.

I sure fixed things good this time, she thought dejectedly. *Mikkel hates me, Jay deserts me, I can't stay out of trouble, and now I'm lost in these stupid woods! I just want to go home!*

Something rustled in the bushes nearby and she jumped, startled. Glancing on down the hill, she saw something that looked like a roof. Making her way closer, she saw signs of habitation. A wood pile, an outhouse, clothesline strung between two trees. *Whose place is this?* Then she saw a cabin.

Two dogs near the cabin leaped to their feet and broke into the loudest barking she had ever heard. In that same moment, she realized where she was. *Mr. Adams' cabin!*

The two huge dogs were coming at her. She knew that they were mean and that they would tear her to pieces. The only thing she could think of in that moment was to get to the lake. Surely help would be there, and she could get away.

Streaking around the woodpile, she dodged past a small shed, down past the garden, and around the cabin.

The dogs were closing in. She glanced back and realized that she would never make it to the lake. She could almost feel their teeth ripping into her legs.

Just ahead was a good-sized birch, and although she never remembered later just how she did it, she suddenly found herself clinging to the lower branches about ten feet up the smooth bark. The dogs bounded against the tree and continued barking.

She saw a flashlight come on in the cabin, and a few minutes later the door banged. She heard the old man's mutterings before she saw him, his hair askew and clutching his long, wicked-looking gun.

"Blackie! Prince!" The old man grated out. "Whatcha got there?" He shone the powerful beam of light into the tree. Jodi tried to call out, but her throat constricted with fear.

"So! A snooper! A thief!" Mr. Adams yelled, cocking his gun. "I'll teach you to come around here, buster! Yessir!" With that, he pulled the trigger.

Jodi was still trying to call out to him when she saw the gun go up to his shoulder. The blast shook the tree, and Jodi, her eyes squeezed shut, slipped down the smooth bark and fell into a heap at the base of the tree. She felt the glare of the flashlight on her, and she braced herself for the next shot, which was sure to find its mark.

"Come on, get up," he was saying gruffly. "I didn't mean to hurt you, only scare the daylights out of you. Come on!"

Jodi struggled to her feet, her mind still spinning and great sobs shaking her body. Still she could not speak.

Mr. Adams took her silence for stubbornness. "Well, what do you have to say for yourself? Sneakin' around my place in the middle of the night! I've heard about all these robberies! I'm not so dumb. Where do you live?

97

What's your name?"

She took a big breath and straightened up beside the tree. "I'm not a thief," she said, her voice still shaky. "I was out in a boat, and I got lost! My name is Jodi Fischer, and I'm staying with the Evanses."

"The Evanses!" He looked at her again. "So you say! I say you're lying!" He grabbed her arm. "Come on, girl! I'll take you over there right now, and we'll just see!"

With a sigh of relief, Jodi let herself be towed down to the dock. She climbed into a small outboard motorboat and held Mr. Adams's gun for him while he started up the motor.

He must be crazy, she thought, shaking her head. The motor roared to life, and he took back his gun. Then they left the cove and rounded the point of land. She strained to see the canoe, but she couldn't see anything.

A cold wind bit through her T-shirt, and she wished she had worn her jacket. She dreaded awakening Mr. Evans. *Here I am, causing more trouble,* she thought. *I wonder what they will say, and what happened to Jay?*

They pulled up to the Evanses' dock and climbed out. Mr. Adams still held his gun as he herded her up the hill. A few minutes later he pounded on the door of the cabin, and they waited in silence. Jodi heard voices, rustlings, footsteps, and then the door swung open.

Mr. Evans peered out into the night. "Who—what— Jodi! What are you—"

"Sneakin' around my property in the middle of the night!" Mr. Adams roared behind Jodi. "Does she belong here? I'm callin' the police! With all these rob—"

"Jodi!" Mrs. Evans came up behind her husband and drew the shivering girl into the kitchen, where a kerosene lamp glowed brightly.

"Come on in," Mr. Evans invited the old man in a

puzzled tone of voice.

"What's this all about, Jodi?" he asked, scratching his head.

"You won't get nothin' straight from that sneak, I tell you! She—" Mr. Adams said.

"If you don't mind," Mr. Evans interrupted him, "I'd like to hear what Jodi has to say!"

With a grunt, Mr. Adams leaned against the wall.

Jodi shook her head. "Well, last night I saw Mikkel going out of the tent, and I followed her to the dock, and I knew she had taken the boat out somewhere. So when she came back, I asked her where she had been, but she wouldn't tell me." She cleared her throat.

"So Jay and I decided to follow her," she went on, "and Jay got a canoe, and when she left during the night, we got up and followed her over to this clearing behind Mr. Adams's place. Mikkel met her father. I fell out of the bushes, and he ran off. Mikkel got mad at me and said she was running away, too."

Jay came into the kitchen rubbing the sleep from his eyes. Jodi looked at him in surprise.

"After that, I couldn't find Jay, so I walked down the hill and came out at Mr. Adams's place. His dogs almost tore me apart, and I had to climb a tree. Then he came out and shot at me! He thought I was a thief! He almost scared me to death!" She glanced at Jay and caught a smirk just leaving his face. "I'm sorry I went without your permission, Mr. Evans," she said, sniffing. "I—I guess I wasn't thinking straight."

Mr. Evans turned to Jay. "Well, Jay, what do you have to say for yourself? You should have come to me!"

Jay's eyes were heavy with sleep. "Me? I don't know what she's talking about! I haven't left the cabin all night!"

Jodi was so stunned her mouth dropped open and her blue eyes widened. But her surprise soon changed to anger. *Leave me to take the rap alone! Why, the—*

Mr. Evans turned to Mr. Adams, frowning. "I appreciate your bringing Jodi back," he said evenly, "but the next time you use a weapon on someone, *I'll* call the police and have them take it away from you! Can you find your way out, or would you like me to show you?"

Mr. Adams sputtered and grumbled as the door was opened and he was ushered out into the night.

"What about Mikkel?" Mrs. Evans asked suddenly. "Is she here?"

"Jodi," Mr. Evans said wearily, "go and see."

At the tent, Jodi pushed back the flap and gasped. Not only was Mikkel gone, but her sleeping bag and suitcase were missing, too! She ran back to the cabin.

"She's gone!" Jodi exploded. "All of her things and everything! She must have run away like she said she was going to do!"

Mrs. Evans cried out, and Mr. Evans rubbed his forehead. He frowned at Jay. "I will deal with you later," he said. "For now, you're grounded from using the boats. Get your shoes on. We'll see if we can find her." He began pulling on his boots, and Jay whirled to go to his room.

Jodi sat at the kitchen table near Mrs. Evans.

"You better go to bed and try to get some sleep," Mrs. Evans said, patting her hand.

Jodi shook her head. "I couldn't sleep."

Jay ran through the kitchen, pulling on his boots and throwing on his jacket. Then he and his father were gone.

"Oh, I hope they find her!" Jodi exclaimed.

Mrs. Evans nodded. "Let's pray about it, Jodi!" Her

100

fingers closed tightly over Jodi's as she led in prayer.

She smiled as she lifted her head. "Well, now that you can't sleep, would you like some hot chocolate? It won't take long to get this fire going." She laid the fire and lit it. Then she poured some water into the kettle and set a cup and the chocolate mix on the table.

"Did you get a chance to talk with Mikkel?" she asked Jodi with a smile.

Jodi shook her head. "No, I didn't. I said I was sorry for eavesdropping, but she was so mad she wouldn't listen. I guess I fell out of the bushes just as her father was about to go with her."

"So Mikkel didn't accept your apology."

Jodi sighed. "She was really mad. She said she never wanted to see me again, and all I did was mess things up for her! I wanted to help so much! Nothing ever turns out right for me!" She sniffed and buried her face in her hands.

Mrs. Evans poured hot water into the cup. "That looks so good, I think I'll have some myself." She got her own cup and sat down. Slowly she stirred her chocolate, and Jodi watched the brown liquid swirl in the cup.

"You know, Jodi," she said in her soft, direct way, "I heard once that if you have a cupful of sweetness, that no matter how hard someone bumps it, only sweetness can come out." She paused. "Jesus said that it isn't the things that a man eats that makes him dirty, but what comes out of his mouth. And another Scripture says that out of the abundance of the heart, the mouth speaks."

Jodi looked up. "I know all those things! I know what I should be doing, but things just pop out of me. I can't control what I say!"

Mrs. Evans smiled. "I think every person has struggled with that problem. Even the great King David prayed and asked God to set a watch on his lips. But the real problem is attitudes and thoughts. Whatever is in your heart and mind will come out. Selfishness, jealousy, anger, hatred, all of those things come out in your words." She sipped her drink.

"It's like weeding, Jodi," she continued. "You can cut off the tops of the weeds with your hoe, but that won't stop them. They have roots. You have to pull the roots out."

Jodi nodded. How many times had her mother told her that when she had tried to get by with a quick weeding job in their garden at home?

Mrs. Evans sighed. "I know it's hard work, but you have to get those roots. And the same thing is true in your heart and mind. Jesus gives us the power to root out those thoughts of hatred and selfishness and rebellion. All we have to do is allow Him to cleanse our lives, and then we plant the good seeds of God's Word in our minds." She paused and glanced at Jodi. "I'd say you have some gardening to do, Jodi," she said softly.

Jodi blinked and nodded. "Yes, I guess so. Thanks for reminding me, Mrs. Evans." She was struggling to keep the tears from flooding down her cheeks. "I guess I will try to get some sleep. Thanks for the hot chocolate."

"Good night, dear," Mrs. Evans replied. "Before you go to sleep, though, I'd like you to read two Scriptures. I'll write them down for you. Talk about some good seeds—these would be dandy to plant in your mind." She scribbled the Bible references down on a slip of paper and handed it to Jodi, kissing her good night.

So tired she could hardly stumble out to the tent, Jodi lifted up the flap and crawled in. It seemed scary and lonely without Mikkel. Turning on the flashlight she had found in the cabin, she dug out her Bible and read the two passages.

"Psalm nineteen fourteen, 'Let the words of my mouth, and the meditation of my heart, be acceptable in Thy sight, O Lord, my strength, and my redeemer.'" She turned to the back of her Bible.

"Philippians four eight, 'Finally, brethren, whatsoever things are true, whatsoever things are honest, whatsoever things are just, whatsoever things are pure, whatsoever things are lovely, whatsoever things are of good report; if there be any virtue, and if there be any praise, think on these things.'"

She shut the Bible with a yawn and crawled into her sleeping bag. "Lord, please be with Mikkel and keep her safe," she whispered in the darkness, "and help me to—" But then her eyes fell shut and she was asleep.

The roar of a plane woke her the next morning. She scrambled out of her sleeping bag and poked her head out of the tent. Mr. Evans, just returning from the woodpile with his arms heaped up with wood, grinned at her.

"Are you awake?" he called. "Pancakes are being served! You better rise and shine!"

"Did you find Mikkel?" she called back.

He shook his head. "No, but we found the boat across the lake near the main highway. She must have hitch-hiked. I've already called the police on the CB this morning."

Jodi slipped out of the dirty clothes she had slept in last night and put on her last clean pair of jeans and a blouse. She tied on her tennis shoes and then reached for her jacket. But it was gone! She looked around the tent and saw Mikkel's jean jacket lying crumpled underneath her sleeping bag.

She lifted it out and shook it. "She must have taken mine by mistake," she said, shaking her head. "And mine was a new one!" Her mother had reminded her before they got on the plane not to lose her jacket—it would serve for school next fall.

"If I don't get it back, I'll be in hot water when I get home," she mumbled as she threw back the flap of the tent and crawled outside. It was cloudy, but the clouds were high.

In the cabin, she washed her face and then sat down at the table. Jay and Mr. Evans were wolfing down pancakes as fast as Mrs. Evans could make them.

"Good morning," Mr. Evans said with his deep voice. He passed her the plate of pancakes. "We had an irate call from Mr. Adams this morning. He said several of his tools were missing, and he's calling in a plane to fly him out. He wants to report to the police in person. I'm afraid you are suspect number one unless the real thieves are caught."

Jodi's blue eyes widened and her fork paused in mid-air. "Me! But—but he's just a crazy old man! He's probably just misplaced those things!"

After breakfast, Jodi went back out to the tent to roll up her sleeping bag and pack her suitcase. On the trail, she met Jay.

"Thanks a lot, Jay," she said in a low voice, "for what you did for me last night! I was beginning to think you were all right, but I was wrong! You're about as smart as a turkey!"

"Drop dead!" he retorted angrily and strode on past her. Jodi went to the tent and thumped her sleeping bag and slammed down her suitcase lid. Then she caught

104

sight of the slip of paper Mrs. Evans had written on last night. Slowly she picked it up and looked at the Bible references.

Isn't this just what she was talking about? Jodi asked herself. She rocked back on her heels. *Anger, selfishness, hurting other people? Could it be that most of my troubles on this trip are because of my words?* She thought of Stanley, MaryAnn, Mikkel, and now Jay.

Slowly she finished packing, and then she went to sit on the steps of the cabin, breathing deeply of the clear, pine-scented air. She cradled her chin in her hand.

Desperately she wished she could begin all over again. *But what is past is past,* she thought. *What can I do now? Let's see, I'm going to have to start using my brain if I'm going to get anywhere on these mysteries!* She glanced at her watch. *And I only have two hours!*

She thought back to the airport and the men who chased Mr. Smith. He turned up later, too, at the Neilsons', at Mr. Burke's plane, and then he followed her and Mikkel. Then those guys at the cannery. Loredo. He had come to Lucy Lake! Why? Was he a part of the gang of thieves? Were they the ones who stole the Eskimo painting, too?

Again she came back to the question, Why had Loredo been at Mr. Adams's cabin? Was the gang using it as a hideout? Suddenly she wanted to look around the old man's cabin. What would she find?

Mrs. Evans opened the door. "Church will be on in a few minutes," she said.

Jodi jumped and then stared at Mrs. Evans. "What?"

Mrs. Evans repeated what she had said.

"Oh, your church program on the radio!" Jodi exclaimed. "I had forgotten this was Sunday! I'll be right in." She went to the tent, got her Bible, and then returned to the cabin.

Mrs. Evans was tuning in the radio, and the others sat around in the living room. Jay was sitting on the floor, leaning against the couch, his long legs stretched out in front of him. On his face was a belligerent grimace that said *I'm not listening to that today!* Jodi plopped down on a stool by the window and looked at the radio.

The songs lifted her spirits, but she hardly heard the preaching. Her mind was busy thinking of the mystery, wondering how Mikkel was doing, and planning a trip down to Mr. Adams's cabin. Partway through the sermon, a plane roared over the cabin and Jay jumped up to see who it was.

"Mike," he said when he returned. "The air taxi. Probably taking old man Adams out."

A little later, Jodi heard another plane overhead. Everyone jumped up and ran outside. A green and yellow Cessna with the State Troopers insignia on the door was just coming up to the dock. Mr. Evans tied up the plane and two uniformed policemen got out.

"Hello," they said, shaking hands with Mr. Evans. "We would like to ask you some questions about the airplane you have seen on the lake. Could you describe it? Have you seen any of the passengers?"

Mr. Evans nodded. Then he described the red plane. "I didn't get close enough to see the pilot or the other man in it, but I believe Jodi saw someone."

"Yes, I did!" Jodi said eagerly. She told them about the tall man with the long hair and how he had got off at Mr. Adams's cabin.

"Thank you," the tall, blond officer said. "Could you tell us about Mr. Adams and what happened last night?"

Jodi nodded and explained what she had seen and heard at his cabin. The other policeman was taking notes.

He looked up. "Thank you. Could we go over there and talk with him? Could we borrow your boat?"

"Sure!" Mr. Evans said. "But you won't find him home. He just left this morning to make a report to the police."

"Well, we'll look around his place anyway," the tall policeman said, getting into the boat. "We'll be back soon."

They were soon out on the lake. Jodi sighed and turned back to the cabin, wondering if she would ever find out the answers to this mystery.

Just then she crashed suddenly and violently into someone going up the path. She gripped the other person to steady herself. Then she looked up and saw it was Jay. His face was dark, and his eyes sparked angrily.

"Why don't you watch where you're going?"

She looked down, batting her long lashes and fighting back the angry retort that had surfaced. Suddenly she wasn't angry, only sad.

"I'm—I'm sorry," she said huskily, "Oh, Jay, let's not fight anymore! I was talking to your mom last night, and she said I had a lot of weeding to do!"

He looked at her, surprised. "Weeding?"

A trace of a smile flirted over Jodi's lips. "Well, maybe I should say *rooting*." Then she told him what they had discussed the night before.

He turned his head away. "Oh," he said when she had finished. "Sounds like Mom."

She went on up to the cabin and began helping Mrs. Evans prepare dinner. Mrs. Evans greeted her, and Jodi, glancing toward her, gasped! There was a picture just beyond Mrs. Evans' head, newly hung on the wall. It was the painting of the Eskimo children!

107

9
Captured!

Jodi stepped over to it and touched it. Yes, it was the one painted by Mikkel's father!

"It's really nice, isn't it?" Mrs. Evans asked, pausing as she mashed the potatoes.

"Where—where did you get it?" Jodi asked, her mind whirling.

Mrs. Evans smiled. "From Mikkel. She asked me to keep it for her. There's something strange connected with it. She said I should keep it safe."

"When did she give it to you?" Jodi was still staring at the picture as if she were afraid it would disappear if she looked away.

"Just yesterday," Mrs. Evans replied. She set the bowl of potatoes on the table and dished up the vegetables. Then she put on the moose roast and called the others in for dinner.

"What's the matter, Jodi?" Mr. Evans asked her with a smile. "You look like you've seen a ghost."

The family gathered at the table, and Jodi sat down and bowed her head as they said grace. Then she stood and took the painting from the wall where Mrs. Evans hung it. She turned it over, but there was just cardboard backing behind it.

"The backing had been torn a little when she gave it to

me," Mrs. Evans said. "I repaired it and found that old frame for it."

Jodi replaced the painting and sat down. "That picture is really getting around," she said, helping herself to the meat. "Mikkel gave it to me several days ago, it disappeared from my bedroom at the Neilsons', and now it turns up here!"

"Really?" Mrs. Evans exclaimed. "It seems there *is* a mystery about it! Oh, I do hope Mikkel is all right!"

After the delicious dinner, topped with fresh rhubarb pie, Jodi began helping clean up the kitchen, but Mrs. Evans stopped her.

"You're not doing dishes just before you go home," she said, giving Jodi an affectionate hug. "Jay will help with these. You go on out and enjoy Lucy Lake for the last time!"

Jodi smiled at her appreciatively and couldn't help grinning at Jay's scowl. "Thanks, Mrs. Evans. I would really like that!"

"Just don't be gone too long," Mr. Evans called from the living room. "Mr. Neilson should be here in about an hour."

"I won't!" Jodi called back as she flew out the door and down the path to the lake. The police airplane was just starting up.

"Did you find anything?" Jodi called to them.

The blond officer rolled down his window. "No, we didn't. We'll let you know if anything turns up." With a wave, they were gone.

Jodi put on her life jacket and got into the small green rowboat. With long, powerful strokes she was soon out on the lake, the bow pointing toward Mr. Adams's cabin. She was sure she could find something that the policemen had overlooked. This was her last chance to try to solve the mystery!

A chilly wind lifted her hair and ruffled the lake into frothy waves. She was glad she had worn Mikkel's jacket, but she frowned at the clouds. After she had been out on the lake a short time, rain began pelting the surface of the water.

She glanced at the shoreline. There was the finger of land up ahead with the tall snag at the top. Soon she beached the canoe and entered the woods on the trail she and Jay had taken the night before.

As she climbed up the hill, her mind was busy with the puzzling mystery of Mikkel and her father. She was convinced that Mikkel had known all along more than she had told her. What kind of racket was her father mixed up in? What had he meant about spying on someone? Was it the thieves? How did old man Adams fit in? Had he purposely tried to throw suspicion on her?

She passed through the clearing where Mikkel had met her father, and then she went down the other side of the hill, working her way carefully through the underbrush. It was raining harder now.

As she approached the cabin, she wondered about the dogs. Would they come out at her? She saw the roof of the cabin first and cautiously inched her way forward. Suddenly the woods exploded into sound as the dogs began their racket. She froze, eyeing a good-sized tree nearby. But the dogs didn't come. Working her way up to the cabin, she saw they were tied.

Letting out her breath, she waited, hiding behind the woodpile. Finally the dogs settled down and quietness descended on the clearing. Jodi looked around, watching and listening, keeping hidden behind the pile of wood. After what seemed to her like years, she moved and was about to step out when she heard a plane coming in from the far end of the lake just over the treetops. *It was the red Beaver!*

It landed on the lake, and then all was quiet. Jodi waited, her heart beating wildly. Suddenly she had a startling thought. *Maybe the thieves hide their stolen goods here at Mr. Adams's cabin! Maybe that was why he was so upset when he caught me last night!* But what could she do?

Before she had thought of anything, a tall man stepped out of the cabin and went down to the dock. It was Loredo. Maybe they were going to unload some stolen goods. If only she could get word to the Evanses, and they could call the police!

Hey, Mr. Adams had a CB, she thought excitedly. Poking her head from behind the woodpile, she looked down toward the dock, Loredo was gazing out over the water. Quickly she ducked across the open space and darted into the cabin.

Glancing around quickly, she looked for the CB radio. For a bachelor's home, the cabin was quite tidy. She saw piles of magazines, an easy chair—there it was, beside the chair! She strode over to it and turned it on, expecting to hear the usual static and chatter. But it was dead. She flicked the switch several times. Nothing! Now what?

She glanced out the window and saw the large red plane pulling quietly up to the dock. She realized she should get back to the Evanses and call the police, but would there be time? Could she find where the crooks stored the stuff?

Frantically she glanced into the one curtained-off bedroom, but nothing was there. Then she dashed outside and hid behind the cabin. Over to the left she saw an old cache, a small log building built up on tall stilts with a ladder going up to the small doorway. She knew those were used by trappers in the wilderness to keep animals away from supplies and furs.

It would be the perfect place to hide stolen goods! It was built among the trees just a little beyond the cabin. Jodi darted across the clearing and up to the ladder that led to the small doorway.

She had just started up the ladder when she heard voices coming up the hill! She paused, wondering what to do. If she went on up, she would be in plain sight of the men who were climbing up the slope from the dock.

Gritting her teeth, she scrambled up several more rungs. And then she heard a sound that struck terror to her heart. It was a splintering, creaking sound. The ladder was breaking under her weight! She stopped, her eyes wide with fear and her hands clutching the ladder tightly. She glanced down and suddenly felt dizzy. Just then, she heard voices quite close and then saw Loredo and another man near the cabin. She froze, hoping they wouldn't see her.

Intent on the cabin, they didn't even glance in her direction. Jodi let out a sigh of relief and tried inching down the ladder. But the moment she shifted her weight, the splintering noise came again. The men whirled around, saw her, and began sprinting to the cache with loud yells.

Now she knew she would have to come down and try to get away. She took a step downward, but with a loud splintering crash the ladder gave way and she was falling, falling—

When she opened her eyes, she was flat on her back, looking up into low, gray clouds. It was raining on her face, and her head hurt when she moved it. A man stood near her head, and Loredo was carrying something down the trail.

"This is it!" he said. He came out on the dock, and Jodi saw he had the CB radio, several guns, and an armload of furs. She sat up and moaned, holding her head. The other man was fat with black, frizzy hair. Pushing the stolen things into the already well-filled storage space, he turned to her.

"Loredo, help our snooper into the plane, and let's get going!" He climbed into the pilot's seat and started the engine.

Loredo leaned down and pulled Jodi to her feet. She held her aching head and looked out at the lake, hoping to see a boat coming across the waves. But Loredo pushed her into the plane.

"You—you can't do this!" she stuttered. Loredo jumped into the seat beside her and shut the door.

"Shut up!" he said, flinging his gun in her direction carelessly. She shrank back from him and looked out her window as they taxied away from the dock and then lifted off the lake. In the distance, she saw smoke coming from the Evanses' cabin. Instantly she thought of the warm kitchen, and tears sprang to her eyes.

Last time I'll see that, she thought bitterly, *and I've let them all down!*

The men were laughing about their easy haul.

"Good work, Loredo," the fat man said. "That was a good idea of the boss's to hire you out to work for Adams. You got some inside information so our job was easier."

Loredo grinned. "It was easy. When I heard he was leaving today, I knew it would be wide open for you to come in." He shook his head. "Good thing I stopped to help the old man with a flat that time. It's things like that that get us good contacts."

He glanced at Jodi and frowned. "What are we going to do with her?"

The other man shrugged. "That's for the boss to say."

Jodi looked at him and thought she had seen him somewhere before. But where? She puzzled about it for some time, and then remembered. At the airport! He was one of the men who had stopped Mr. Smith and stolen his briefcase! So how did Mr. Smith fit into all of this? Her head hurt, so she leaned back against the seat and closed her eyes.

Some time later, she felt the plane dipping down, and she looked out the window. They were circling a small lake not far from Anchorage. A few minutes later, they were down. There were quite a few cabins, and planes on the lake, and Jodi was surprised at the brazenness of the gang. When the plane landed at the dock, a man stepped out of a rundown blue van and began bringing out large cardboard boxes.

As soon as Jodi saw him, she knew who he was—the other man she had seen at the airport. Had she heard his name? His hair was receding, and he wore a rather shabby business suit. Jodi thought he looked like a nice grandfather, but his face was hard and his eyes sparked angrily. He flashed a glanced at Jodi.

"Who do you have in there?" he asked as he tied up the plane and they climbed out.

The big man answered with a hitch to his pants. "She was snoopin' around Adams's place," he said. "We'll have to take her down and lock her up with the other one until the boss says what he wants done with her."

They shoved her into the van and then quickly transferred all of the stolen articles out of the plane and into the boxes. Then they loaded the boxes into the van.

Jodi felt helplessly caught as Loredo sat down on the

seat near her and the other two men sat in front. She opened her window and the breeze coming in cleared her mind. They approached Anchorage and soon were in the city. Loredo was talking to the other two men, and Jodi noticed his gun had disappeared.

She edged the window open further and looked out at the people on the sidewalk and in other cars. *If only I could signal someone that I'm in trouble,* she thought desperately. They pulled up for a stop light, and a noisy motorbike sputtered in her ear in the next lane of traffic. She glanced over at the driver. He looked up at her in the same moment, and she gasped. It was Stanley!

10

A Way of Escape

"Stanley!" she yelled, leaning out the window. "It's me, Jodi! Get the police! I'm being kidnapped! Help!" Loredo whirled to her and yanked her back inside. The van started with a jerk, and she was shoved to the floor. Her mind blacked out, and when she came to several minutes later, the van was careening crazily.

"Of all the stupid—" the older man who was driving was muttering as he wrenched the wheel sharply. "Let her scream out to all the world! Why didn't you have her gagged?"

Neither of the men answered. The older man kept looking in his rearview mirror.

"I can't get that brat off my tail!" he exclaimed. "Listen. I'm going to pull in by the cannery, and you guys jump out and grab him! And do something right for a change!" The two men stationed themselves beside the door, ready to jump.

Jodi's heart was thumping madly. Stanley had followed them! *Oh, Lord! Help him to turn away and get the police!* The van screeched around a corner and slowed down while the two men jumped out. Then it rolled on for a few feet and jerked to a stop. The older man climbed back near Jodi and held a gun near her head.

116

"One squeak and you're dead!" he said viciously through clenched teeth. The small revolver shook.

Jodi stiffened on the floor of the van where she was last thrown and heard the sounds of men shouting, Stanley's voice, the crash of the dirt bike, and then several solid thuds.

"OK, let's go." The driver motioned with his gun. Jodi slowly climbed to her knees and then jumped out of the van. The other men were supporting Stanley's limp body between them, and she put her hand to her mouth to keep from screaming. Had they killed him?

The older man's gun was in her back, and they all entered the back door of a long, tumbled down cannery. The building was large and empty, except for piles of boxes near the back. He snapped on a light in one small room to the right and shoved her inside.

It was a small office of some sort, and as Jodi glanced around she gasped. Mikkel was sitting there, tied to a chair! They carried Stanley in and dumped him on the floor and tied his hands and feet. Loredo pushed Jodi into a chair and tied her tightly to it.

"You got some company," Loredo said to Mikkel. "I'm sure you'll have lots to talk about!"

Mikkel ignored him, her round, black eyes on Jodi. The men turned the light off and left the room, locking the door behind them. In the dim light, Jodi could just make out Mikkel's head near the far wall. Stanley began to groan and move around.

"Mikkel?" Jodi said, her voice sounding detached in the semi-darkness. "How long have you been here?"

Mikkel sighed. "I don't know. What time is it?"

"Let's see," Jodi replied. "I left the Evanses' cabin around one o'clock, and was at Mr. Adams's cabin about an hour, and then the ride in. It must be around three."

Stanley rolled over. "Where am I?" he demanded. "Oh, my head!"

"Caught!" Jodi said, frowning. "Caught by the same gang that got me! Why didn't you just see where we were going and then get the police like I asked you to?"

Stanley groaned again. "Last time I'm going to try to be a hero! Just try to rescue a stupid girl!"

Jodi chuckled mockingly. "Well, now, hot stuff! You're really in a fix this time, and mother dear isn't around to bail you out! So all you can do is blame someone else!"

"Oh, dry up!"

"Both of you are acting like spoiled kids," Mikkel said bitingly. "It really helps a lot to sit around and fight!"

Jodi's anger died. Mikkel was right, of course. She thought of her talk with Mrs. Evans and the Bible verses she had read. She sighed.

"You're right, Mikkel," she said in a low voice. "Stanley, I'm sorry. I've been—unkind to you. Will—will you forgive me?"

Stanley grunted.

Jodi glanced toward Mikkel. "What's going on?" she asked. "Are you still mad at me?"

"I'm not mad," Mikkel replied softly. "Not anymore. I've had a lot of time to think. And pray. It wasn't your fault, Jodi. I can't say much because I think they left someone outside to listen in and see if we say anything."

Jodi eyed the area where the door was and strained to hear even the tiniest sound from the hall. But all was quiet.

"Can you tell me how you ended up here?" she asked. "And why you gave the—"

"Jodi," Mikkel interrupted quickly. "I'll tell you all I can. After I left the Evanses' cabin, I rowed across the lake and got a ride to Anchorage. Then I went to the Holmeses', but I know I was being followed. This morning, I was going to take your jacket to the Neilsons', but they got me." She paused. "That's all. I have your jacket here. I saw you are wearing mine. At least we can exchange jackets."

Jodi smiled. "When we get untied, that is. I thought Mr. Adams was in with the gang that is stealing things from cabins, and I went over to his place and got caught when they came to rip off his cabin. I saw Stanley on the way over here, and he followed the van and got caught, too. What were you doing driving that bike, Stanley?"

Stanley rolled over. "Just trying out a friend's of mine! Isn't there some way out of here? All the detective stories I've ever read, they always find some way out!"

Mikkel sighed. "This isn't a book, and we aren't detectives," she said wearily. "I'm so tired of sitting in this chair! I wonder what time it is now."

They all made a guess and then fell silent. It bothered Jodi that they couldn't talk freely. She squirmed in her chair and it squeaked beneath her. Suddenly she had an idea.

Deliberately she squeaked back and forth on the rickety old chair. Harder, harder—then the legs folded underneath her with the sound of splintering wood. She fell on her side and was dazed for a few seconds.

"Jodi, what in the world!" Mikkel exclaimed.

Jodi kicked and the ropes on her feet were loose. "Hey, it's working!" she panted. "Now, just the back." She fell on the chair back and heard more splinterings. Kicking her feet and wiggling her hands, she found the rope getting looser and looser. Finally she stood up, free! The chair lay in pieces at her feet.

"See?" she said triumphantly. Suddenly she glanced at

the door. There was the sound of footsteps approaching. They paused outside the door and then moved off down the hall. She went to Mikkel and untied the rope that held her. Several broken fingernails later, Mikkel stood and stretched,

"Oh, that feels so good! Thanks, Jodi!"

"Hey, you guys!" Stanley muttered from the floor. "What about me?"

For a second, Jodi thought it might be nice to leave him tied and gagged, too, but she knelt with Mikkel at his back and worked on his ropes. Soon they were all walking around the room.

Jodi carefully tried the door, but it was padlocked from the outside. Then she boosted Mikkel up to a tiny window high on the wall, but she came down, shaking her head.

"It's too small to even get my head through," she whispered. "And it's made of that strong plexiglass stuff."

Jodi sank down to the floor and leaned against the wall. "Let's sit down and think," she said dejectedly.

"All I can think of is food," Stanley remarked, still roving around the room.

"Oh, you had to say it, didn't you?" Jodi asked, "I'm so hungry I could eat my shoes!"

They talked for some time, and finally Stanley settled down on the floor near Jodi. She thought of the plane that should have been taking her and MaryAnn home, and a big lump formed in her throat. *Home!* What she wouldn't give to be home right now!

What was going to happen to them? Would the gang go so far as—as murder? She tried to get more comfortable on the floor and think of something else. But another question haunted her. *If that did happen, am I ready to meet the Lord?* And the answer was no. *I belong to Him but—* She turned her head into the crook of her arm.

"Oh, Lord," she whispered softly, "I've got my back against a wall again. When will I learn I can't do anything without You?" She paused, sniffing.

"Except sin. I'm pretty good at that. Lord, I know You must see such awful things I've been allowing in my heart and mind. Jealousy—forgive me for being jealous of MaryAnn. And anger and hatred. Pride is there, too, isn't it? How could I feel superior to anyone when I've gone so low myself?"

She wiped at her wet cheeks. "No wonder I've had trouble with my words! Oh, Jesus, just cleanse me and help my words to be kind and helpful! I don't know what else to say, except thank You!"

Feeling lighter and at peace, she crumpled down in a little ball on the floor and fell asleep. It was darker when she next awoke, and she was cold and sore. She moved a little and felt someone's warm body. Jodi curled up close and went back to sleep.

The key jingling in the lock woke her. Light once more filtered in the tiny window, and Jodi, opening her eyes, realized morning had come. She heard men's voices and sat up. Stanley moved beside her. Mikkel had pillowed her head on Jodi's jacket a little distance away.

The door opened and the older man walked in, turning on the light. "They got loose from their chairs," he said to two men who followed him in. "I heard that, but they didn't get out. Well, boss, what are we going to do with them?"

Mikkel and Stanley sat up, blinking their eyes against the bright light.

Jodi blinked, too, and tried to make out the men as

121

they came in. There was Loredo, and the fat man. At first she thought she couldn't be seeing right as the last man came in. *It was Mr. Burke!*

He took several steps into the room and shut the door behind him. Wearing a business suit, his dark hair combed back neatly, he looked more like a respectable businessman going to work. But his piercing blue eyes glinted dangerously, and Jodi knew her first impression of this man had been correct.

He glanced at Jodi and Stanley. "Get them in the corner and watch them!" he barked to Loredo. Loredo jumped as if he had been stung by a bee. Then Mr. Burke whirled to Mikkel and grabbed her by the arm.

"You! Sit here!" He plunked her down on a chair. "Now, you can save yourself and everyone else a lot of unpleasantness if you would tell me what you have done with that painting, my dear Miss Pokiak. I must remind you I'm not playing games!"

Jodi shivered at his words. His chilling attempt at being polite was more frightening than any of the harsh words he had used. She realized that here, indeed, was a dangerous man.

He leaned closer to Mikkel, but she stared straight ahead, her face set stubbornly. He slapped her and straightened up.

"You will learn to answer me," he said. "I know how to make you talk! We got your father last night, and we'll bring him in and torture him!"

Still Mikkel did not budge. "You don't have him," she gritted out between her teeth.

Suddenly Burke whirled to Jodi and striding over to her, he yanked her to the desk and pushed her down on it.

"OK, snooper," he said, leaning close to her, "it's your

turn. Are you going to talk, or do we have to persuade you?" Casually he took a long knife from his belt and began running the blade over the corner of the desk.

She drew back, her heart banging in her ears. Her mouth felt like someone had crammed a wad of cotton in it, and beads of sweat popped out on her forehead.

"I—I don't know anything," she croaked out.

"Oh, yes, you do!" He grabbed her arm. "You had the painting once. What happened to it? Where is it now?" He touched her arm with the blade of the knife.

"I don't know!" she heard herself screaming. She tried to pull her arm away, but he held it tight. "I've only seen it once since it was stolen!"

"Where?" he screamed in her face. He brought the knife up to her neck.

"You don't know them!" Jodi began, and then she choked out, "The Evanses! Leave me alone!"

As soon as the name was out, he dropped his arm and returned the knife to his belt. With a grin, he turned to Loredo.

"Who do we have here? Stanley Neilson! He may just bring a nice sum for ransom! OK, let's go." He strode to the door. "Don't bother tying them up. They won't get away. And if it's not there, my girl, we will be back!"

Jodi crumpled off the desk as the door slammed, her face in her hands and sobs shaking her body. How could she have told him? Then she felt Mikkel's arm around her shoulders.

"Hey, listen," Mikkel said softly in her ear. "It's not your fault. Now we have to find a way out of here. Right?"

Jodi looked up through her tears and saw Mikkel's bright eyes. She sniffed and wiped off her face.

"A—a way out?" she repeated. "But we can't get out!"

123

Mikkel smiled. "Yeah, I know." She looked up at the ceiling. "But we haven't tried one way yet."

"What way?" Jodi sat up and followed Mikkel's gaze at the ceiling, half expecting to see a trap door. But there was nothing. She heard Mikkel's soft laugh, and then she smiled.

"Oh! You mean God's way! Mikkel—do you believe?"

Mikkel's eyes were moist. She nodded. "I believe Jesus died for me," she said, "and that He hears when we pray."

"Let's pray right now!" Jodi replied and bowed her head. "Lord, we need a way out of here. Please help the Evanses and be with them. And show us what we should do. In Jesus' name. Amen."

Then, to her surprise, Mikkel prayed, too. "Dear Jesus, I believe You died for me. Please forgive my sins. And help Daddy wherever he is. Thank You. Amen."

Jodi looked up, her blue eyes sparkling with tears. She hugged Mikkel.

"That's all very nice," Stanley said behind them, "but now let's get out of here!"

Jodi glanced all around the room, and then her eyes came back to that small window. She wondered if she could break it. Picking up a piece of broken chair, she pulled another chair below the window and began to pound on it.

"Oh, Jodi! That won't work!" Stanley grumbled.

She stepped down off the chair and began looking for something heavier. Suddenly she heard someone at the door, rattling the padlock. They all froze and listened. Was it the men coming back? But the rattling stopped, and all was quiet. Jodi stepped over to the door.

"Is someone there?" she asked nervously.

"Who is in there?" called a man's voice back. Jodi

thought she recognized it, but she couldn't remember from where.

"Jodi Fischer, Stanley Neilson, and Mikkel Pokiak," she replied. "We were captured by a gang of thieves! Can you get us out?"

"One moment, please," the man replied faintly. Then there came the sound of sawing. It seemed to Jodi he took forever, but then the sawing stopped and the door swung open.

And there stood a small, dark man with a neat moustache.

11
A Test by Fire

"*Bonjour!*" Mr. Smith bowed slightly and entered.

Jodi took a step back, staring at him. "Mr. Smith! What—"

He held up his hand. "Please. Call me Pierre. What am I doing here? I am rescuing you. In exchange for some information, of course."

Jodi hesitated. "How do we know whose side you're on? Who are you, really? How did you know we were here?"

Pierre stepped further into the room and closed the door, tucking a tiny hacksaw into his suit pocket.

"I am a private detective, hired by a museum in France," he replied. He brought out his wallet and displayed an identification card.

"I followed the men here this morning, but I didn't know someone was in here until I heard pounding on the window. As to whose side I am on—"

"Let's just get out of here!" Stanley said suddenly, heading for the door.

"Not so fast, my boy!" Pierre said, moving quickly to stand in front of the door. "First I must know what you did with the painting, Mikkel. And where that man Burke and his gang went so quickly in their airplane."

Mikkel shook her head. "I gave it to Mrs. Evans to

keep safe for me. We're wasting time! The gang went out to get it, and the Evanses are in danger!"

"Then let's go!" Pierre opened the door. "But I must find the painting, so I am taking you with me. If it is not where you say, I will hold you responsible!"

Stanley pushed past him and darted for the door. Jodi picked up her jacket from the floor and stepped out into the hall, pausing to look at the pile of crates at the back of the room.

"That must be the stolen goods," she said to Mikkel. The Frenchman was dragging someone down the hall. Jodi smiled as she saw it was Loredo—tied and gagged. Depositing him in the office, Pierre tied him to the desk and shut the door.

"That will hold him until the police get here," he said with a hint of a smile behind his moustache. Then he led the way to his rented car. They all piled in, and Pierre roared away from the cannery.

Downtown, he suddenly pulled to the curb and turned to Stanley.

"I will leave you off here," he said. "You will call the police and tell them about the stolen goods at the cannery. I am sure you can get home."

Stanley slowly opened the door. "But I want—"

Jodi pushed him out. "Call the police, Stanley!" she said. "It doesn't matter what you want!"

"You're not my—" Stanley began, but Pierre screeched out into traffic, and Jodi slammed the door. She looked back at the small, dark boy and kept mouthing "Police" at him for as long as she could see him.

Pierre drove to Hood Lake and stopped abruptly close to a dock where a small green plane was tied up. A man jumped into the plane and started the motor. Pierre held the door for Mikkel and Jodi, and then he jumped in and shut it. The pilot taxied out onto the lake.

"Lucy Lake!" Pierre yelled above the noise of the propellers. The pilot nodded, obtained permission for take-off, and pointed the small plane into the sky.

"Where is—who did you say—the Evanses' place?" Pierre asked Jodi, leaning back toward her.

"On the far side of the lake, opposite the highway," she yelled back. The pilot nodded again. "But I think it would be best to land down the lake a way and taxi in closer. It would be quieter."

Pierre relayed that to the pilot.

Jodi leaned back and looked out the window. She glanced at her watch. *Eight thirty!* Her stomach told her in complaining tones that she had missed both dinner and breakfast.

It was chilly in the plane, so she flung on her jacket. Something felt funny as she leaned back, and she wondered if a tissue or piece of paper had gotten out of her pocket and into the lining. She felt the pocket. No, there was no hole. She shrugged and looked out the window again.

Lucy Lake came into view some time later, and Jodi's heart began racing. Would they be in time to help? How could they rescue the Evanses? How could they get the painting?

The pilot set down the plane near the far end of the lake and began taxiing quietly toward the cabin, following the shoreline. Jodi squirmed at the delay, but Pierre seemed calm. As they approached the Evanses' cabin, she leaned forward.

"Let's get out along here," she said, indicating the beach. "It's not far to the cabin from here."

The pilot glanced at Pierre, and he nodded agreement. The plane nosed into the beach, and Pierre got out first, stepping on the pontoons and then leaping to the sand. Jodi and Mikkel followed him.

"If we're not back in half an hour, go get help," the small Frenchman said to the pilot. He nodded and cut the engine, glancing at his watch.

Jodi led the way through the woods. When they came in sight of the cabin, Pierre touched her arm.

"Sneak up behind," he whispered. "We'll try to see what is going on by looking in the windows."

Carefully, her heart pounding loudly, Jodi led the way up and around the cabin, keeping low and behind the thick underbrush. They heard men's voices as they drew near to the windows in the living room. Pierre stood slowly and peered in. Jodi held her breath.

He sank down. "Burke and two other men are in there, talking," he whispered.

Just then the back door opened, and someone came out. Jodi peered around the bushes. It was Jay. Pierre leaned to her.

"Go talk to him," he said. "Tell him you have to get the painting. He can bring it out, surely. Hurry!"

Jodi's feet felt like lead, and her head ached. She still wasn't sure that Pierre was on the level. Maybe he was working for another gang. Maybe his card was a fake. But she pushed down her doubts and crept up behind the woodpile where Jay was gathering an armload of wood. He turned to go back to the cabin.

"Jay!" she whispered as loud as she could. He stopped and looked around. "Behind the woodpile. It's Jodi! I have to talk to you!" He dropped the wood in his surprise and whirled around.

"Come closer," Jodi said, hoping no one was watching from the cabin. "Pretend you're picking up the wood again." He recovered and slowly bent to pick up the wood.

"What's going on, Jodi?" he asked. "Where have you been?"

"I don't have time to tell you," she replied. "Just listen and do as I say. You are in terrible danger! Those men in the cabin are desperate criminals, and they are going to try to steal that picture Mikkel gave your mom! The one of the Eskimo children, hanging in the kitchen. You have to bring it to me right now. Hide it under your shirt, or something. Then get a gun. I'm afraid we'll need one!"

Jay nodded, and Jodi noticed his face had turned white. Quickly he turned and with a few sticks of wood in his arms, he sprinted up to the cabin and disappeared inside.

Jodi was still staring at the cabin when she heard something behind her. Turning with a jump, she bumped into Pierre and Mikkel, who had crept up to the wood-pile.

"That took long enough!" Pierre said, his face twisted with impatience. "Is he getting it?" Jodi nodded. The door of the cabin banged shut and Jay was soon beside them. Pierre drew them all back into the bushes.

"Did you get it?" he asked Jay.

Jay nodded. "Yeah." He drew the painting out from under his shirt. "I had to go into Mom's bedroom. She took it out of the kitchen. What's going on?"

Pierre ignored the question and took the painting from him. Ripping the frame from the picture, he carefully ran his finger along the edge of the cardboard backing.

Jodi glanced at Mikkel. Her eyes were wide, and her face was pale.

"What is he looking for?" Jodi asked her.

Mikkel, as still as a carved wooden figure, stared at

Pierre as he carefully removed the canvas from the cardboard. Finally it was free, and he looked behind the canvas. In motions of great surprise and anger, he looked again, feeling with his hands.

"It's gone!" he said angrily. He turned to Mikkel. "It's gone! Your father lied to me! Where is it?" He grabbed her shoulder and shook her.

She pulled away from him, her eyes blazing. "I won't! I won't tell you! No one will ever find it! It's gone! It's already caused too much trouble! You can go back to your museum and tell them you couldn't find it!"

"What are you talking about?" Jodi nearly shouted. She grabbed Mikkel's arm.

Mikkel turned to her. "One of the old masterpieces was stolen from a museum in France," she said. "I think it was a Rembrandt. Anyway, my father got it somehow and hid it behind this picture. But—"

"Very interesting!" A cold, hard voice interrupted her from behind them.

Jodi and the others whirled around. Burke was standing just behind them, holding a gun. His older accomplice appeared beside him, and then the fat man.

"Let's go to the cabin," Burke ordered. "I would like to hear more about that painting!" He motioned with his gun. "And no funny little tricks!" He shouted as Pierre began reaching toward his pocket. "Mac, grab his arms. I'll see to the rest of them!"

Jodi then remembered hearing the older man's name at the airport. Mac twisted Pierre's arms behind him and forced him toward the cabin. Pierre, his face red and his moustache jerking in agitation, let out a stream of angry French words.

Jodi stepped into the familiar warm kitchen and was prodded on into the living room. Tears stung her eyes at

131

what she saw there! Mr. and Mrs. Evans were seated in chairs, their feet and arms tied securely! Mrs. Evans, her white hair disheveled and her face pale, smiled as Jodi came in.

"Oh, Jodi! You are all right!" she exclaimed. "And Mikkel, too! How are you, dears?"

Jodi blinked her long lashes and stepped over to Mrs. Evans and gave her a quick hug.

"Hey! Get away from there!" the fat man shouted. He pushed her to the couch while Mac tied Jay and Pierre.

Burke grasped Mikkel's arm tightly. "Well, I see we are all cozy in here. I have business with this one in the kitchen. I'm sure she'll tell me what she's done with the painting." He pulled her to the kitchen.

"You touch her and I'll—" Mr. Evans yelled after him, but the fat man slapped him.

"You'll keep your mouth shut!" he snarled, nervously fingering his revolver. He paced up and down the room while sounds of tussling came from the kitchen.

"Mac! Get in here!" Nelson cried. The older man dashed to the kitchen and the tussling stopped. Jodi heard Burke's questions and the silence after each one. She winced when she heard them slap Mikkel.

Frantically she glanced around. She had to do something! It hadn't even been half an hour since they left the plane, and the pilot would never get the police here in time! She couldn't even trust Stanley to have notified them!

At the end of the couch, near the wall, was the CB radio. She heard the low chatter coming from it. When the fat man's back was turned, she edged closer to it. Finally she reached up and turned on the mike. She saw Mr. Evans's nod of encouragement.

Burke was yelling in the kitchen, and the other man's

132

back was turned, so Jodi quickly took the mike, pulled up her knees, and hid it down beside her. She pushed the "on" button.

"Breaker! Breaker!" she said breathlessly into the mike. The fat man turned, and she laid her head on her knees. When he paced back to the window, she spoke again into the mike.

"KGN-two fifty calling anyone. KGN-two fifty calling—" She broke off as the man swung around and paced back to her. She held her breath as he stared at her and then went back to the window. On the wall was a piece of paper that had all the CB code numbers on it, and she looked at it, pressing the "on" button again.

"Ten thirty-three!" she said, her mouth right next to the mike. "Ten thirty-three! Ten two hundred* at Lucy Lake! Ten two hundred at Lucy Lake!"

The fat man whirled and looked at her. Then, striding over, he yanked her to her feet.

"Boss!" he yelled when he saw the mike. "This kid's been calling for the cops on the CB!"

Burke raged into the living room. He grabbed the mike and threw it to the floor. Then he pulled the CB from the wall and smashed it. In a fury he grabbed Jodi.

"Come with me!" he ordered. "We've got some business to do before those cops come!" He pulled her into the kitchen and pushed her into the chair.

"But—but I don't know anything!" Jodi said. Mac slapped her hard, and tears sprang to her eyes. She looked at Mikkel. Her face was fiery red, but her eyes were defiant and bright.

"Now," Burke said, "one of you two knows what happened to that painting! I want that information, and I

---

* 10-33—Emergency; 10-200—Police needed.

want it now!" His eyes were wide with a wild look in them, like an animal that is cornered.

Neither girl said anything, and Jodi braced herself for the slap she knew was coming. But Burke turned to the wood stove, and lifting off the lid, he stirred the fire. Something in his movement was sinister and frightening. Jodi shrank back from him.

Burke picked up the poker and lowered it into the fire, "When this comes out," he said slowly, his face red and twisted with anger, "it's going to be very hot. And I'm going to lay it on Jodi's pretty face. And her face will never again be pretty. So you better talk now and talk fast!"

Jodi gulped, her blue eyes wide with fear. She glanced at Mikkel, and Mikkel looked down. Suddenly a verse she had learned a long time ago sprang to her mind. *What time I am afraid, I will trust in Thee.*

Her throat felt like someone was strangling her, and her heart beat a staccato in her chest. She tried to pray, but she could only watch in horror as the poker was raised from the fire, glowing red. The thought came swirling through her mind, *He's really going to do it!*

"Please! No! I don't know!" She heard her voice screaming, and somewhere a man's voice was yelling, too. Mac grabbed her and held her tightly. The glowing poker waved through the air near her face, and behind it she saw the insane, evil, leering face of Mr. Burke!

12
Mr. Pokiak's Story

"OK! OK!" It was Mikkel's scream filling the kitchen. Suddenly the room revolved and became black, and Jodi slumped down in her chair. When she came to several seconds later, Mikkel was shaking her shoulder.

"I need your jacket, Jodi," she was saying softly. Burke and Mac were pressing close, greed filling their faces. It took several minutes for Jodi to comprehend what Mikkel was saying, but finally she took off her jacket and handed it to her.

She watched as Mikkel tore out some hand stitching in the bottom of the lining, and then pulled out a small eight-by-ten piece of canvas. She handed it to Burke.

Burke grabbed it and spread it out on the table. Jodi saw there an old painting of an English street, and an old man sitting by the doorstep of a house. This was the valuable Rembrandt painting! She had even seen a photograph of it in the encyclopedias at home!

Burke was smiling. "Ah, at last! It's mine! Worth a few grand to the right people. Wasn't it worth it, girls? You could have saved a lot of difficulty by just telling me right away."

The fat man had stepped into the kitchen to look over Burke's shoulder at the painting on the table. And right at that moment, the door of the cabin opened and shut.

Jodi looked toward the door and heard Mikkel cry out.

"Father!"

The three men whirled around. A heavyset, dark-skinned man with a bushy moustache and black hair stood near the door, a long rifle pointed at Burke and his gang. His dark eyes darted from one person to another.

"You will put down your guns," he said softly, moving the rifle a little. "*Paniga,*" he said, glancing at Mikkel, "go untie those in the other room, then we will have rope to tie these dogs."

Mikkel sprang up, and Jodi followed her to the living room. Mr. Evans nodded toward the bedroom.

"There's a knife in there," he said. "Quickly! On top of the dresser!"

Jodi found the knife and quickly cut the ropes holding Mr. and Mrs. Evans, Jay, and Pierre. Then they all hurried to the kitchen where Mr. Evans and Pierre securely tied up the three men. Mr. Pokiak motioned to the painting on the table.

He nodded to Mikkel. "Hand me the painting, daughter. It is the only way." He looked at Mr. Evans. "I am sorry. I do not wish to cause trouble, but you must give me the painting."

Just then Pierre stepped forward. "Forgive me, sir," he began, making a stiff little bow, "but the painting belongs to the museum in France I represent. I received a letter from a Mr. Pokiak, saying he would contact me and I would find the painting hidden behind one of his own."

Mikkel's father nodded. "I am Mr. Pokiak. I have secured the painting for you. I understand there is a reward?"

Pierre nodded and removed a wide belt from around his waist.

Opening a zippered compartment, he counted out a stack of bills and handed them to Mr. Pokiak. Then he bowed and replaced the belt. Going to the table, he gently picked up the painting. "Now, if you will excuse me," he said,

But Mr. Pokiak stayed in front of the door. He peeled off some of the bills and laid them on Burke's lap. "There!" he said forcefully. "I have paid my debt, and I no longer have anything to do with you!"

Pierre moved toward the door again, but just then they heard the roar of a plane overhead.

"The police!" Jodi squealed. Mr. Pokiak whirled to the door, but Mikkel caught his jacket and clung to him.

"Father! No! You must listen!" she cried. "Please don't keep running away! Everything will turn out if you will just face up to things!"

Burke was struggling against his ropes. "Take this money, Pokiak, and let me free! We'll be square!"

Mr. Evans appeared in the kitchen with a rifle. "No one is leaving," he said, his voice icy. "And that includes you, Pierre. Now, Jay, go bring those policemen in!"

Jay dashed out of the cabin and soon brought up the two policemen.

"What's going on here?" they asked Mr. Evans.

Mr. Evans shook his head. "From what I gather, these men here were trying to secure a stolen masterpiece. And this gentleman is from France, hired by the museum to bring the painting back."

"Also," Jodi said, "these guys here, Burke and his gang, are the thieves that were stealing from the cabins on the lakes. The stolen stuff is hidden in a cannery in Anchorage where we were held last night!"

Pierre bowed to the two policemen. "*Bonjour,*" he said. "I am very happy now, and may I go, please? I have just bought the painting from this gentleman. Good day."

"Not so fast, buddy," one of the policemen said. "Why don't we all start at the beginning and tell the whole story. Then we will see who goes where." He glanced around. "Who would like to begin?"

"I think you should," Mikkel said to her father.

The Eskimo man sat down heavily. "Yes, Mikkel. I am lucky to have such a fine daughter as you." He sighed.

"I am a poor man, but I can do one thing. That is paint. There is no work in our village, and when my wife died, Mikkel and I leave to go to the big city. There I find work. I paint my fingers off for this big crook!" He wagged his finger at Burke.

"Then, after work, big boss invites me to a saloon where they gamble in the back. I will show you. He has many rackets in town. This game, he says, is on the house. Gambling, it is my downfall. Soon I am in deep. Burke says I have to work off my debt for the gang. He sends me on errands. I have to do the dirty work."

He sighed again. "I see no way out. Then one time I got to be friends with another guy. Someone was out to get him, and he got shot. I came to his place right after that, and he was dying. He told me about this painting. "It's worth lots of money,' he said, and I could have it. He told me where he hid it, and then he died." He rubbed his moustache.

"I got the painting, but I didn't tell anybody. I wrote to the address I saw on the back and told them I would sell them the painting, and I would meet their man at the airport. But the Boss got wind of it and got me drunk and found out everything—everything except where I hid it. He threatened me with my life, and I laughed! Then he said he would hurt my *paniga*, my little girl. So I

138

ran off and hid. I put the painting behind one of my own and gave it to my daughter before I left. She gave it to this other girl. That is all, except when I couldn't find Mikkel, I came back to Lucy Lake and I find them all here."

There was silence in the cabin, and then the policeman turned to Jodi.

"And, now, what is this about stolen goods?" he asked.

She told him all that had happened to her, while the other policeman took notes. Finally they untied the men and handcuffed them.

"You are not free to leave the state," the policeman told Pierre. "You will come down and give us a written statement. We will examine your papers, and we will need this for evidence and safekeeping." He lifted the painting from Pierre's grasp.

Pierre's moustache jerked up and down. "Delay! Delay! I would just like to go home!"

Everyone chuckled, relief flooding their faces.

The policemen loaded Burke and his men into the large police plane. Mr. Pokiak was taken as well, but the officer assured him of a light sentence if he would testify against Burke.

"We'll need a written statement from you, young lady," he said to Jodi. "So come down to the office later. You will probably have to come up for the trial, too, as a witness."

Jodi frowned. "But I have to go home! How can I be here?"

The policeman shrugged. "Fly up here, I guess. The state will pay your way."

"Oh!" She grinned at the happy thought, and Mrs. Evans put her arm around her shoulders.

"And when you come, dear, you will have to visit us again," she said.

They watched the police airplane leave, and then Pierre's chartered green plane landed and taxied up to the dock.

"I went for the police like you said to," the pilot told him, "but they were out here already. Everything OK?"

"Just fine," Pierre replied a little grumpily. "Come along, girls."

Mikkel climbed in the backseat, but Jodi hung back, thinking of her empty stomach and Mrs. Evans's delicious cooking. Mr. and Mrs. Evans gave her a final good-by hug, and she turned to get in the plane. But someone was pulling on her arm. It was Jay. His hazel eyes twinkled, and a happy light shone on his face.

"Good-by, Jodi," he said, extending his hand. She shook it and smiled up at him.

"So long, Jay," she said. "I'll write and maybe see you again soon."

"I hope so! Tell MaryAnn to write, too. I wanted you to know I got my weeding done this morning."

She laughed and reached up to give him a kiss on his cheek. Then she scrambled into the plane. Mrs. Evans handed in her suitcase and purse, and then they were in the air, waving to the three small figures far below.

Jodi shook her head and glanced over at Mikkel. "They are really neat people," she said. "But I'm still wondering about some things, Mikkel. Did you know the Rembrandt was behind your father's painting all the time?"

Mikkel smiled. "No, I didn't. I knew Daddy was mixed up in something bad, but I didn't know what was going on. I never did trust that Mr. Burke. It was his voice I almost recognized that night on the boat!" She

140

paused. "And it was his gang that followed me in the black car. Then, when they saw you coming out of the house with his picture—"

Jodi nodded. "They figured I had it, and they followed me! It must have been them who tried to break into the Neilsons' that night. But who finally got the painting? And how did you end up with it?"

"Daddy called me soon after you left that day and asked about the picture," Mikkel said, looking down. "I told him I had given it to you, and he was really upset. He went to the Neilsons' house the next day and told Stanley a story and offered to buy it."

"I figured as much," Jodi muttered. "So that was your father driving away! I thought it was Mr. Sm—I mean, Pierre. They both have dark hair and moustaches. But how did you know to meet your father by Mr. Adams's cabin, and what was he doing there?"

Mikkel sighed. "He called me just before we came out to the Evanses', so I told him where we were going. He knew the gang was operating out there, so he went to spy on them, hoping to catch them and turn them in. He brought the masterpiece with him, but he didn't feel safe with it in case the gang caught him, so he gave it to me again. That was the first night I met him. He told me all about it then, and I was really frightened and I wanted him to turn it in."

"Then when you got back to the Evanses'," Jodi continued, "you took the masterpiece from behind your father's painting and sewed it into my jacket. Why did you do that?"

Mikkel gazed at a small village they were passing over, and then she turned back to Jodi.

"Actually, I didn't sew it in your jacket until I got to the Holmeses' house," she replied. "All I could think of

141

was to get it away from here. I was going to write to you and tell you, and you could turn it in to the police down in Canada. That way it would never be traced to Daddy, and it wouldn't cause any more trouble." She sighed.

Jodi shook her head. "Well, it is all going to turn out all right, I know," she said. "But one more question and then I'll stop. Why did you take that book of matches I found on the trail?"

Mikkel turned away quickly and for a long time she wouldn't answer. Finally she turned to Jodi, her black eyes moist.

"Perhaps you don't understand," she said in a very low voice. "My father—he is all I have in the world. He is on parole. I recognized the matches as his because of the writing on the back. I was afraid you would turn it in to the police, and he would be suspected of the robberies on the lake. Please forgive me. I—I only did what I thought I should."

Jodi laid her hand on Mikkel's arm. "Of course! I was wrong to suspect you! I was all mixed up inside then, but I think God and I have things straightened out now. Oh, look! Anchorage! Man, am I hungry! Hey, Pierre! Let's get a hamburger!"

The pilot set down the plane on the lake, and Pierre laughed.

"I think it will be just as fast to take you home," he said. "And cheaper, too!"

They got into his rented car and dropped Mikkel off at the Holmeses'. Mrs. Holmes ran out to envelop Mikkel in her arms.

"Oh, you're safe! We were all so worried!" she said. "Can't you come in, Jodi?"

Jodi shook her head. "I'd better get on over to the Neilsons'. I don't know when they have scheduled the

142

flight home."

Mrs. Holmes smiled. "Well, I'm sure you'll get a big welcome! Tell your parents hello for me!"

Jodi waved as Pierre screeched away from the curb.

She thought of Mrs. Holmes's words on the way to the Neilsons'. Feeling tired and hungry, she thought, *A big welcome! That's what I deserve!* She pictured everyone running out to welcome her, to hug her, and to cater to her needs.

The first thing she noticed at the Neilsons' a little later was that the driveway was full of cars and there were a lot of people around. Men were loading equipment into their cars, two ladies were talking with Mrs. Neilson, there was another knot of people near the door, and three or four more scattered over the lawn, snapping pictures or writing notes in their notebooks.

Jodi assured Pierre she could walk up the drive and got out of the car. No one seemed to notice her as she approached the door. She spotted Mr. Neilson and Stanley by the door, talking with two men and a lady and laughing. The lady took a picture of Stanley and his father. Then everyone was calling out good-by and their thanks, and heading toward their cars.

Jodi paused on the sidewalk, her suitcase feeling like it had an elephant in it. She set it down and wiped her forehead.

"What in the world is going on?" she asked a smartly-dressed young man who hurried past her. The man only gave her a nod and was gone. She looked toward the door, but Mr. and Mrs. Neilson had just gone inside and the door was shut.

13

Sweeter Than Honey

Slowly Jodi walked up to the big fancy door and pressed the doorbell. Tears were just below the surface, and she sniffed as the door was opened. It was MaryAnn.

"Jodi!" she said. "You're home!"

"Hi, MaryAnn," Jodi said in a small, strangled voice. She stepped inside and glanced around. There were more strangers inside—a man in the living room, a lady in the kitchen talking with Mrs. Neilson.

Jodi sighed, suddenly more weary than she had ever been in her life. "What's going on, MaryAnn?" she asked.

MaryAnn smiled, her brown eyes laughing. "This is Stanley's greatest hour!" she exclaimed. "He's a hero, Jodi! He's going to be on television and in the newspaper and everything! Man, is it ever exciting!"

Jodi swallowed, her head spinning and her knees nearly collapsing underneath her, "Television? How come?"

MaryAnn laughed again. "Come on in. He'll tell you. Look, Aunt Phyllis! Jodi is home! She wants to know why you're going to be on television, Stanley!"

Stanley turned to her and grinned jauntily. "Oh, I see you're back from the lake. I called the police and told them about the cannery. I guess half the stolen goods in

Alaska were there, plus a lot of other incriminating stuff. Man, this hero stuff is great!"

Jodi gulped. Her head was spinning faster now, and somewhere deep inside she felt resentment and jealousy rearing their ugly heads.

"Did—did you tell the police about the gang going out to Lucy Lake? We got in trouble out there, you know. Burke and his gang captured everyone."

Stanley waved his hand indignantly. "No, I didn't think that was necessary. After all, Pierre was with you. The important thing was to tell them about the cannery!"

And now anger gripped her. Her heart was pounding in her ears, and a screaming voice surged up inside her. She clenched her fists and her face turned red as she looked at Stanley's laughing, mocking face. But then something stronger, something more powerful checked the angry words that were forming on her tongue.

She swallowed and looked around. She knew she had to get away from Stanley, alone in her room to deal with her feelings before God. She took a step toward the stairway, stumbled, and then all was black.

When she next came to, she was lying on her bed in the large, beautiful room she had shared with MaryAnn. Something cold was on her forehead, and she reached up to feel a damp washcloth. MaryAnn bent over her, and Mrs. Neilson bustled across to the bed.

"Is she coming around?" Mrs. Neilson asked.

MaryAnn nodded. "Jodi? Are you all right?" She began rubbing Jodi's hand.

Jodi smiled a little and shook her head. "I seem—to be making—a habit of this," she said.

Mrs. Neilson patted her shoulder. "Is there anything I can do for you, dear?" she asked solicitously.

Jodi looked up at her. "I—yes, I guess there is, Mrs.

Neilson. I haven't had anything to eat since yesterday noon. I guess I fainted because I'm so hungry."

"Oh, my!" Mrs. Neilson exclaimed, "You poor thing! Why, of course I'll get you something! You just rest here, and I'll send a tray down in a little bit. Imagine! Since yesterday—" Muttering, she left the room.

MaryAnn sat on the bed next to her. "What happened, Jodi?" she asked. "Are you strong enough to tell me? We heard you were missing, and then Stanley said you were going out to the lake."

"Just be glad you weren't along," Jodi replied, grinning at MaryAnn. "It wasn't your style of fun." Then she told her all that had happened to her. Finally she lifted MaryAnn's bandaged finger.

"How is your finger, MaryAnn?" she asked. "Isn't it healing right? Is that why we have to go home?"

MaryAnn sighed. "It's doing OK. Dad and Mom just got upset and wanted us to come home. How's Jay, Jodi?"

Jodi hesitated. "Well, he's fine—now. He got his weeding done this morning."

Just then Mrs. Neilson brought in a tray filled with good things to eat—turkey sandwiches, Jello salad, sliced fresh tomatoes, deviled eggs, milk, and a big piece of lemon meringue pie.

"Weeding?" MaryAnn asked, puzzled.

Jodi nodded and in between bites told MaryAnn what Mrs. Evans had shared with her. "Last night I confessed it all, MaryAnn, and Christ is the one who does the weeding! I'm so glad He's cleaned up my life! I'm sorry for the things I've said to you, MaryAnn. I was so jealous of you I couldn't see straight! Will you forgive me?"

MaryAnn blinked. "*You?* Jealous of *me?* Why, Jodi, I've been jealous of you! I'll forgive you. Will you forgive me?"

"Of course!" Jodi exclaimed, and suddenly she was laughing and crying and hugging MaryAnn at the risk of toppling her lunch tray. "Anyway," she went on, "Jay had some weeding to do, too. And he's gotten his life right with the Lord. He said he wants you to write to him."

"All right!" MaryAnn said softly, her brown eyes shining.

Jodi finished her lunch and handed MaryAnn the tray. "Would you mind taking this back upstairs?" she asked. "I think I'll get a shower and take a little nap. Don't let me sleep too late, though. I have to go down to the police station to file a report."

MaryAnn nodded. "OK. By the way, we're flying home tonight at nine fifteen. That is, *if* you can stay out of trouble long enough!" She laughed and ducked out the door as Jodi made a lunge for her.

Jodi felt like a new person when she awoke several hours later and put on the clean clothes MaryAnn had washed and dried for her while she slept. Then Mrs. Neilson drove her and MaryAnn and Stanley to the police station.

Jodi was filling out the lengthy report when she glanced up and saw the same smartly-dressed young man she had seen on the Neilsons' front lawn that morning.

"Ah," he said, smiling at Stanley, "we meet again! Find any more crooks?"

The policeman taking Jodi's report looked up. "Finding crooks! This young lady captured the crooks!" He laughed, but instantly the young reporter was all ears, and he took notes eagerly as Jodi retold her adventures.

Then he took her picture and promised she would share in the story they had already gotten from Stanley.

"Oh, I'm so glad you're getting the recognition you deserve!" MaryAnn said, giving her a hug as they went to the car.

"Deserve?" Stanley remarked belligerently. "I'd like to know what she did that was so great!"

More than you did, smarty! was on the tip of Jodi's tongue, but she clamped her mouth shut. Swallowing her pride, she smiled over at him as they drove through the city.

"Thanks for calling the police," she said meekly, "I knew I could count on you to do the right thing."

Stanley looked at her, baffled. He opened his mouth as if to say something and then closed it again and turned to look out the window.

When they got home, he stopped her on the stairway, just before she went down to her room.

"Hey, Jodi," he said. "What's happened to you? Where's the old fighting spirit?"

Jodi laughed and gripped his arm. "Maybe I learned some things, Stanley."

Stanley pushed his glasses up on his nose. "Oh, yeah? Like what?"

She frowned and thought for a little. "Well, for starters, that it's a lot nicer to say pleasant words than cruel, angry words. And that it's only God who can give you the strength to do it."

"That's pretty good for starters," he said. "You know, Jodi, I might like you after all."

Her blue eyes sparkled. "I know I like you, Stanley. Once I got myself out of the way." She turned and went on down the stairs, humming a tune.

MaryAnn came up behind her and gave her a squeeze.

"That was nice," she said softly. "And I've got a verse for you. Proverbs sixteen, verse twenty-four. I just read it this morning. "Pleasant words are as an honeycomb, sweet to the soul, and health to the bones.'"

That night, just after dessert was served in the Neilsons' formal dining room, there was a ring at the door. Mr. Neilson went to answer it, and Jodi heard him exclaim, "Well, Mr. Pokiak! And Mikkel! Come on in!" She jumped from her chair and went to greet Mikkel.

Mikkel's round face was wreathed in smiles, and her dark eyes were alight with joy. Mr. Neilson invited the visitors to the living room, but they said they could only stay for a few minutes.

"I'm so glad to see you," Jodi said to Mikkel's father with a smile. She glanced at Mikkel. "I told you everything would turn out all right."

Mr. Pokiak beamed. "Mikkel's friends at the Native Fellowship raised my bail! We are going now to their meeting." He glanced affectionately at his daughter. "I have much to learn about this—this Christianity, but Mikkel will show me."

Mikkel handed Jodi a package. "I want you to have this, Jodi," she said in her soft voice. "It's not much, but you will remember us with it. Don't open it until you're on the plane!"

Jodi flushed and accepted the package, curious about what it could be. The Pokiaks turned to leave, but before they could open the door, the bell rang once more. Mr. Neilson raised his eyebrows and opened the door.

A short, dark man with a moustache stood on the doorstep.

"Mr. Sm—I mean, Pierre!" Jodi exclaimed. She invited him in and introduced him to MaryAnn's aunt and uncle.

He bowed to them. "I am free at last to leave the country and go home," he said in short, clipped words. "But before I go, I must thank you for your part in helping to recover the stolen masterpiece." He paused and dug in his shirt pocket, pulled out an envelope, and handed it to Jodi. "For you, Mademoiselle! The museum wired my salary, and I feel I must reimburse you for the difficulties and sufferings you have endured."

He also handed an envelope to Mr. Nielson. "You must see that Mr. and Mrs. Evans receive this to replace their radio set. It is—how do you say it?—a business expense? Once more, I say *au revior*." With another short bow, he was gone.

"Well, Jodi," MaryAnn said, giving her a gentle nudge, "open it! What is in it?"

Jodi slowly opened the envelope. She heard MaryAnn gasp as she drew out two five-hundred-dollar bills.

"A thousand dollars!" MaryAnn burst out. "What are you going to do with it, Jodi?"

Jodi's thoughts swirled as she stood and stared at the money.

"We must be going, Jodi," Mikkel was saying. "Good-by, and I hope we can write—"

"Wait!" Jodi clutched Mikkel's arm. "This money! Mikkel, I want you and your father to have it. You can go to art school and everything! Really! I want you to have it!" She held out the money, but Mikkel just stared at it.

Jodi laughed, her blue eyes dancing. She reached over and pressed the money into Mikkel's hands.

Tears spilled out of Mikkel's black eyes and coursed down her round cheeks. "Oh, Jodi! What can I say? How can I thank you?" She looked at her father. "Do you remember, Daddy? How we prayed for money for the lawyer?" she said softly.

Mr. Pokiak smiled and nodded. He turned to Jodi. "But, my daughter," he said, his voice rough with emotion. "We cannot take this from you. You keep it. It is yours."

But Jodi shook her head and refused the money.

Mikkel threw her arms around her in a wordless good-by, and Mr. Pokiak shook her hand.

"We will not forget," he said. "You are my second *paniga*, and someday we will meet again."

Jodi felt warm, salty tears streaking down her cheeks as she waved good-by.

"That was the best reward I could ever get," she said softly.

Later, after fond farewells and a few tears, Jodi and MaryAnn buckled their seat belts and felt again the mighty thrust of power as the jet soared into the sky bound for Seattle. The setting sun filled the sky and the Inlet with multi-colored shades of pink and purple with the long, low mountain, Sleeping Lady, silhouetted black in the bright glow.

Jodi sighed and leaned back in her seat. She was tired, but it was a happy, satisfied kind of tired. Her eyes drifted shut, but MaryAnn jiggled her arm.

"Hey, sleepyhead!" she said, smiling. "I'm dying to see what Mikkel gave you. Come on, open it up now!"

Jodi smiled and picked up the package that lay on her lap. She felt it. It was about the size of a piece of paper and bumpy along the edges. Finally she could stand it no longer. She tore off the wrapping.

"Oh!" MaryAnn exclaimed, and Jodi felt tears on her cheeks once more.

There, framed and beautiful, lay the painting of the laughing Eskimo children in the blizzard, and in one corner was the name *J. Pokiak*.